"You're very young, aren't you?"

Morgan's eyes were somber as he lifted a finger to trace the outline of her painted lips.

"But I'll get older," Lyn stated. She moved closer to him. "And I'm old enough," she added huskily.

"One moment you act like a spoilt teenager," Morgan said in an exasperated voice, "then the next like a woman with a world of experience. So how am I supposed to treat you?"

"Like a woman," she answered in furious urgency. "Please."

"Oh, Lyn." Lifting his hand, Morgan put it behind her head, his fingers twisting strands of her hair. His eyes holding hers, he pulled her slowly toward him, then lowered his head to kiss her.

SALLY WENTWORTH began her publishing career at a Fleet Street newspaper in London, where she thrived in the hectic atmosphere. After her marriage, she and her husband moved to rural Hertfordshire, where Sally had been raised. Although she worked for the publisher of a group of magazines, the day soon came when her own writing claimed her energy and time.

Books by Sally Wentworth

HARLEQUIN PRESENTS

HARLEQUIN ROMANCE

Don't miss any of our special offers. Write to us at the following address for information on our newest releases.

Harlequin Reader Service
P.O. Box 1397, Buffalo, NY 14240
Canadian address: P.O. Box 603,
Fort Erie, Ont. L2A 5X3

SALLY WENTWORTH

taken on trust

Harlequin Books

TORONTO • NEW YORK • LONDON
AMSTERDAM • PARIS • SYDNEY • HAMBURG
STOCKHOLM • ATHENS • TOKYO • MILAN

Harlequin Presents first edition August 1991
ISBN 0-373-11390-0

Original hardcover edition published in 1990
by Mills & Boon Limited

TAKEN ON TRUST

CHAPTER ONE

IT WASN'T often you saw a Rolls-Royce in a kibbutz.
The stately car, still sleek and gleaming despite a thin
layer of dust, drove slowly into the central square
attracting, like some mechanical Pied Piper, a comet
trail of brown-limbed, dark-haired children who ran
excitedly in its wake. Their shouts attracted Lyn's
attention where she sat in the shade of the veranda,
and she looked up from her sewing to watch the car.
Some VIP, she guessed, so full of his own importance
that he had to flaunt his wealth and status in such a
humble place.

The Rolls pulled up in front of the administration
building and a man got out, a man so different from
what she had expected that Lyn's eyes widened in
surprise. With light brown hair, lean and muscular, his
strong face tanned by the sun, and so tall that he had
to unfold himself from the car, the man stood for a
moment, hands on his hips, looking around him with
unconcealed interest. He's a Brit! Lyn thought,
recognising with instinctive certainty an indefinable
air about him that told her the stranger was a fellow
countryman. She glanced quickly at the car for
confirmation, but there was no GB plate on the back.
His eyes raked the buildings round the square and
some primitive premonition made her draw back into
deeper shadow, not wanting to be seen. The man's
eyes, hidden behind dark glasses, swept on, seemed to

linger for a moment when he came to her building, but then continued their scrutiny. Only when he had looked all round him did he go into the office, taking the steps two at a time in a long, easy stride.

Lyn relaxed with a heavy sigh, not realising how tensely she had held herself. She resumed work on the boy's shirt she was mending, but almost immediately her eyes went back to the office as she wondered who the man was and what he wanted. Not many Britons came here, and if they did it was usually to stay at the guest house, to experience a short taste of kibbutz life as part of their holiday. But this man certainly hadn't looked like a holidaymaker: there had been purpose in the way he had scanned the square and had strode into the office. Again a tremor of uneasiness ran through her, but Lyn shook it off; just because a man who looked British had arrived, it didn't mean that it was anything to do with her. And besides, no one, not even her mother or father, knew she was here.

'Hey, isn't that a Rolls-Royce?'

Dave had returned from working in the fields and stood gazing at the car. His tanned body, in just a pair of shorts, was liberally splashed with white paint.

Lyn nodded, but said, 'What on earth have you been doing?'

He gave her one of his wide, happy grins. 'Painting the avocado trees white to stop the sun shrivelling them up.'

They both laughed at the absurdity of it, but then Dave said, 'Let's go look at the car,' and started to move towards it.

'No!' Lyn spoke more sharply than she had

intended, and to cover it quickly shrugged and said,
'It's just another car. Aren't you hungry? Why don't
you go and scrub that paint off before we eat?'

He gave her a surprised look but amiably turned and
strolled back. 'I suppose you see cars like that all the
time in England,' he remarked as he came up the steps
to the veranda. 'We don't see so many in the States—
not old ones like that, anyway.'

It hadn't registered before that it was a veteran car,
but now Lyn saw by its square, solid lines that it must
be thirty or forty years old—not an antique, but a
collector's item for all that. It was painted silver and
looked to be in immaculate condition. But the fact that
it was old made her wonder even more about its owner.

Behind her, Lyn could hear Dave singing lustily as he
showered. The tune was a pop song that was at least two
years out of date, but then, he had been at the kibbutz far
longer than Lyn's six months, and the latest Western
music took a while to reach them. He was a volunteer,
sent over to Israel by his university to spend time in the
kibbutz and learn its way of life, and he had liked it so
much that he had stayed on. All the young volunteers who
came to live and work here were placed with 'kibbutz
parents', and because Lyn could speak only English she
had been placed in the same house as Dave.

Other workers were coming in from the fields and
walking across the tree-shaded grass of the square to
look curiously at the car. What sort of man would own
such an eye-catcher? Lyn wondered. An exhibitionist?
An egotist? Whatever he was, he was still in the office,
so his business must be of some importance.

With sudden impatience at her own unease, Lyn got

up and went into her bedroom. It was very small and
basically furnished, but there was a hand-basin with a
mirror over it in the corner by the window. Dave was
still in the shower, so she had to make do with a wash
before she put on a clean dress and tied a matching
kerchief peasant-fashion over her long, fair hair,
bleached even lighter by the sun. When Dave was
ready they walked together over to the big communal
dining-hall, among the first people there as Lyn had to
work in the kibbutz restaurant again that evening.

They sat with some other English-speaking young
people and were soon deep in conversation, so that
Lyn didn't notice Naomi, the ten-year-old daughter of
her 'kibbutz parents', until she came up to the table.

'Hi, Naomi.' Dave put his arm round the child. 'Are
you going to come eat with us?'

'No. I have a message for Lyn,' Naomi said in her
careful English. 'She is to go to the office, please.'

So her premonition had been right. Tension filled her
again as Lyn got slowly and apprehensively to her feet.

'Would you like me to come with you?' Dave asked
in quick concern.

'No, of course not.' She managed a smile. 'It's
probably nothing important.'

She followed Naomi out of the hall, her shadow
lengthening in the dying sun as she walked, tall and
slender, across the grassy square. There were two
people waiting for her in the office: the man who had
arrived in the Rolls, and Amos, the duty member of
the governing committee of the kibbutz. After a swift
look at the stranger, Lyn turned her whole attention on
Amos, who gave her a reassuring smile.

'It is all right, Lyn, you are not in any trouble. You have a visitor. Does that surprise you?' She didn't answer and he went on, his voice gentle, 'Perhaps it should surprise you, for it seems that your parents have been looking for you. They have asked this man, Morgan French, to find you.' He gestured towards the stranger, who was leaning casually against the wall by the window, his eyes on her, but his face devoid of expression.

'When you came here you told us it was with your parents' permission,' Amos went on.

He didn't reproach her for telling a lie, but the question was there in his voice.

'I'm over eighteen,' Lyn said defensively. 'I don't need their permission. And they couldn't have cared less where I went.'

'Well, it seems that they cared enough to send someone to find you,' Amos reminded her. He stood up. 'I think it will be better if I let Morgan explain. I will talk to you again tomorrow, Lyn.' He turned to shake hands with the man, who was no longer a stranger. 'You can talk here and, when you have talked, Lyn will show you the guest house and where you can eat. *Shalom.*'

'Thank you. Goodnight.'

When Amos had gone Lyn turned to face Morgan French. 'What are you—some kind of detective?' she demanded, belligerence hiding uncertainty and hope. 'A private eye? Only I thought private eyes were supposed to be discreet; you could hardly call yourself that when you drive a Roller.'

He had straightened up when Amos left, and now

Morgan came to perch on the edge of the desk, looking her over assessingly. He had taken off the sunglasses and she saw that he had blue eyes, the intense blue of a summer sky. His mouth thinned and he gave a small smile. 'I don't do this professionally, if that's what you're getting at. I happened to be in this area and your father asked me to look out for you.'

His voice was strong, like his body, and probably his personality, too. But Lyn seized on one word. 'My father? It was he who sent you to find me? Not—not my mother?'

'No. I've never met your mother.'

She had been sure it was her mother who had sent him, and to learn that it was her father instead came as a shock. Morgan saw that she was busy with her own thoughts and didn't speak until Lyn said, 'How did you know I was here?'

'I didn't. I've been enquiring at all the kibbutzim in this area. And if you want to know how your father knew you were in Israel, then you'll have to ask him that,' Morgan said shortly as she opened her mouth on the question. 'Maybe he hired a detective,' he added wryly.

Lyn shot him a quick look, wondering at his involvement in this. He didn't look the type of man who hired himself out for a living; his jeans and shirt had designer labels and he wore a gold watch on his left wrist. And somehow he seemed too much of a man to be anything but his own boss. A small frown creased her brow as she said, 'Are you a—a friend of my father's?'

He gave a slight shrug. 'More of a business acquaintance.'

'I don't remember him ever speaking about you.'

He stood up, making her feel short in comparison. 'That's probably because I only met him a few months ago—after you took off.'

'I see. How—how is he?'

'He's fine.' Morgan had caught the vulnerable note in her voice and his eyes settled on her face. His voice gentler, he said, 'He's very worried about you. He misses you.'

Lyn gave a sudden harsh laugh. 'Misses me? When he has his new bride to keep him occupied? I'm surprised he even noticed I was gone!' She turned abruptly away, already regretting her outburst in front of a stranger. She went to the window, but it was dark and there was nothing to see. After a few moments she said, 'I beg your pardon. I—I don't suppose you know anything about it.'

'Only what your father chose to tell me,' Morgan replied easily. 'That you weren't mature enough to cope with his remarriage and that you took off without bothering to say goodbye or where you were going.'

She jerked round to face him, her grey eyes wide and angry. 'Did he say that? That I ran away because I was immature?'

'Isn't it true?' Morgan countered.

Her head came up. 'No. I left because I didn't want to live in the same house as the woman who broke up my parents' marriage.'

'So why come all the way here? Why not just move out of the house into a flat or something?'

'You don't understand,' Lyn said on a petulant note. A thought occurred to her and she said, 'Have you ever met my father's—new wife?'

'Your stepmother? As a matter of fact I——'

'Don't call her that!' Lyn interrupted fiercely.

'But that's what she is, whether you like it or not,' Morgan pointed out, watching her warily.

'Well, I don't like it. I want nothing to do with that woman! She's just a gold-digging b——'

'You don't have to say it,' Morgan broke in shortly, a frown creasing his brow. 'I get the picture.'

Her eyes went swiftly to his face at his tone, and Lyn realised that she had been far too open with someone she hardly knew. 'I'm sorry,' she said stiffly. 'I'm sure you must find all our family problems extremely boring.' He didn't speak and she went on, 'OK, so now you've found me. Now what? Are you going to report back to my father?'

'Yes, but first I think you'd better read this.' And he took an envelope from his pocket and held it out to her.

'What is it?'

'A letter from your father.'

Lyn instinctively put her hands behind her back and clasped them together. 'I don't want to read it.'

'So he was right about your being immature.'

She shot him a fiery glance but took the letter. 'There's a difference between immaturity and—and. . .'

'Obstinacy,' he supplied for her.

A brief glint of amusement came into her eyes, but then they grew sombre again as Lyn looked at the envelope in her hand. 'I'll read it later.'

'Fine. Perhaps you could show me where the guest house is, then?'

'Yes, of course.' Lyn tried to bring herself back to

reality, her thoughts having wandered back in time and space to London and the rows there had been when her parents' marriage had broken up. She and Morgan walked outside, and found several people looking at the car in the light of the lamps. 'Perhaps you'd like to drive your car over.'

'OK. Jump in, it isn't locked.'

Lyn got into the right-hand side passenger seat, and was immediately diverted by the old-fashioned grandeur of the rich upholstery and walnut fascia of the dashboard. 'Mm, nice.' She leant back against the soft leather of the seat. 'Is it yours?'

Morgan shook his head regretfully. 'Afraid not. I came out here to pick it up for a collector friend in England.'

She frowned. 'You didn't come here specifically to find me, then?'

'No, I told you; you were just incidental.'

Lyn didn't quite know how to take that, but it certainly showed which was of most importance to Morgan French. Feeling a little piqued, she sat back in the seat and told him which direction to take—and didn't see him give her an assessing glance and his mouth twist in amusement as he accurately read her expression. They drove over to the guest house where she saw Morgan booked in, then said, 'I'm afraid you'll have to excuse me; I have to work in the restaurant tonight.'

'Is that where I'll be eating?'

'Yes. It's over to the right, near the swimming pool.'

'I'll probably see you there, then.'

She gave a reluctant nod. 'Perhaps.'

She left him and hurried over to the restaurant; she was already late for her shift and it was a point of pride in the commune to always be on time. But Amos must have sent word because there were no reprimands awaiting her. The inhabitants of the kibbutz ate together in the communal dining-hall, but this restaurant was for people staying in the guest house and for any other outsiders who might want to eat there. Lyn worked as a waitress and usually it wasn't very busy, but tonight a large party had come in to celebrate someone's birthday, and she was rushing around almost till closing time. The letter burnt a hole in her pocket but she didn't attempt to snatch a few minutes to read it. She wasn't even sure that she wanted to read it, just as she was reluctant to talk to Morgan French again when he came in for a meal. Both he and the letter represented a world that she had fled from in a turmoil of angry emotion. Here, she had found a completely new world; peaceful, meaningful, its values so different from those she had left behind. Lyn knew instinctively that once she had read the letter nothing would be the same again, even if it was only her own conscience that gave her no peace.

Morgan sat at one of her tables but Lyn asked one of the other girls to serve him. 'Of course,' the girl agreed eagerly. 'Is he the one with the beautiful car? He is beautiful himself, no?'

Lyn supposed he was good-looking in a tough kind of way, and his eyes were especially attractive, but right now she was in no mood to think of Morgan as anything but the bringer of bad news. She managed to successfully avoid his eye and gave a small sigh of relief when she saw him leave. It wasn't till nearly midnight, though, before the people at the birthday celebration reluctantly left. Lyn and the other staff waved them on their way, and then she was free at last to open her letter. After saying goodnight to the others, she turned, not in the direction of her house, but towards the road that led out to the fields.

It was a beautiful night, the moon a perfect crescent in the clear velvet of the sky. She came to the plum orchard and sat on the bank of the irrigation stream, listening to the water, the life-blood of the commune, making a happy, tinkling sound as it flowed along. She sat for some time, savouring the peace of the place, almost afraid to read her father's letter; but with a sigh she eventually took it from her pocket and reluctantly opened it. It was a very long letter. Lyn read it by the light of a torch she'd brought with her from the restaurant, and could picture her father as he wrote it, frowning, angry, but trying so hard to be reasonable and persuasive, not to put down anything that would drive her even further away.

He wanted her to come home, that came across very strongly. He said that he missed her and that he was sorry if his actions had made her run away. His only reproach was for not letting him know how she was. 'Your mother and I are terribly worried about you,' he wrote. Well, at least that's something they still share, Lyn thought with bitter satisfaction. It had been a terrible blow when her father had announced, seemingly out of the blue, that he had met someone else and wanted a divorce after nearly twenty-five years of a marriage that Lyn had always presumed to be happy. At least, she had never had reason to question her parents' contentment.

Her mother had been terribly upset, of course, and Lyn had been completely on her side, but her father had left and, after what had seemed to Lyn only a very short time, her mother had capitulated and given him the divorce he so badly wanted. Lyn and her mother had even moved out of the family house because it had been in Lyn's father's family for generations. Left it in possession of the sleekly beautiful, gold-digging, marriage-breaking. . . Lyn's thoughts seethed with anger as she remembered how her father had actually wanted her to go and live with him and Claire, the woman who had seduced him—a woman only a little more than ten years older than Lyn herself. She had laughed in his face, and told her father that she never wanted to see him or his new wife again, only to be devastated to find that her mother intended to go away to forget, and had made it quite clear that she didn't want Lyn with her. So, feeling deserted and unwanted by both parents, she had taken off and ended up here.

She read on, her father telling her how happy he was now that he was married to Claire, and how he knew that he had done the right thing. That he and her mother had been drifting apart for years. Lyn read that with complete scepticism, wondering at his selfishness and disregard for the hurt he had caused her mother. But, only a few paragraphs further on, she read the shattering news that her mother had married again—to an Australian she had met while on a cruise!

Lyn stared disbelievingly at the sheet of paper in her hand. It was impossible! Her mother had been so terribly hurt, completely shattered, when her marriage had broken up. She had said that she would never trust a man again. She must have married this Australian on the rebound, Lyn decided, and had done it just to show her father that she was still attractive to other men. There could be no other reason. Staring down at the letter, she gave a small bewildered sob. What had her mother been doing on a cruise, anyway? Lyn had been sure that her running away would have made her mother cancel her own plans to go abroad. She had imagined her mother sitting at home, distraught with worry, doing everything she could to find her only child and beg her to come home.

That it had taken so long to trace her should have warned her, Lyn supposed. But now she knew; both her parents were so taken up with their own lives and emotions that they had no time to worry about her. A great rush of self-pity filled her, to be followed by a growing feeling of uncertainty, her once secure world shaken yet again. She felt lost, unwanted, and terribly vulnerable.

'So you got round to reading it?'

Lyn's head jerked round at the sound of a man's voice behind her, and she saw Morgan standing a few feet away. She hadn't heard his approach, but then, her thoughts had been miles away. Without waiting to be asked, he came over and sat down on the bank beside her.

'What are these trees?' He pointed at the dark shadows of the orchard.

'Fruit trees; the ones behind us are all plums.' She turned to look at him. 'Were you taking a walk?'

'No.' He met her eyes steadily in the moonlight. 'I followed you from the restaurant. I thought you might need a shoulder to cry on.'

'You *know* what's in this letter, then?' she asked in surprise.

'Your father told me that your mother had married again, and that he thought the news might upset you—if your reaction to *his* remarriage was anything to go by.'

'Daddy must be more than just a business acquaintance if he told you that,' Lyn said on an accusing note.

Morgan shrugged. 'We get on OK.' He raised an eyebrow. 'And I see that you are upset.'

Lyn turned away. 'You don't think I should be do you? You think I'm immature—isn't that what you called me?' she said bitterly. 'Well, I'm sorry but I can't help it.'

'Aren't you pleased that your mother has found happiness again?'

She laughed harshly. 'That sounds like the "reasonable arguments" my father used to try and persuade me to accept what *he* was doing. No, I'm not pleased. I think she's been driven into this by my father.'

'And your taking off without a word certainly didn't help,' Morgan remarked evenly.

She gave him a hostile look. 'What the hell has it got to do with you?'

'Nothing, I suppose; as you said—other people's domestic problems are always boring. But I thought it would be better to clear the air before I take you back.'

Lyn's eyes widened. 'What do you mean?'

'Haven't you got that far in the letter? Your father has asked me to take you back to England with me.'

'Well, I won't go,' she said immediately, and then bit her lip as she saw Morgan's lip curl mockingly. 'What is there for me to go back to?' she said fiercely. 'Especially now that my mother has remarried. She will hardly want a grown-up daughter around, any more than my father did. I just make them feel old—and isn't that what they're running away from, getting old?'

'Why can't you credit them with genuine emotions?' Morgan asked reasonably. 'Don't you think they're old——' he grinned and corrected himself '—mature enough to recognise their own feelings, their own needs, and to act on them wisely?'

'No,' Lyn answered baldly. Morgan laughed aloud and she gave a reluctant grin, then sighed. 'My parents were perfectly happy for twenty-five years before Claire Jameson came looking for a rich husband—anybody's husband—and seduced my father. OK, maybe my mother and father weren't exactly ecstatic over one another any more, but who expects ecstasy after twenty-five years? They were content, they enjoyed life. We all loved each other, but now all that's gone, and there seems to be more hate around than love.'

'I understand your father asked you to go and live with him when he heard that your mother was going away; he would hardly have done that if he didn't want you around.'

'He probably felt he had to offer,' Lyn answered listlessly. 'But he knew there was no way I would live in the same house as that woman. That's another thing she cost me—my home.'

Morgan was silent for a moment, then said, 'But your father has asked you to go back now, hasn't he?'

'But I won't—not while he's still married to that woman,' Lyn said positively.

'Running away never solved any problem, Lyn. All right, so don't go back to live with him, but at least prove to him that you're responsible for your own life by going back to England and living on your own.'

'What's the point of doing that? I might as well stay here.'

'Are you happy here?' Morgan asked her, his eyes on her face, thrown into relief by the moonlight.

'It's very peaceful.'

'That isn't what I asked.'

After a few moments she gave a small sigh and said honestly, 'It isn't what I expected. I thought it would be far more—more basic, but this is almost like a small town with factories, a concert hall and cinema, and then there's the guest house and restaurant. OK, everybody still shares everything, but it isn't what I expected to find, what I was looking for.'

'What were you looking for?'

Lyn got up and moved restlessly away. 'I don't know, really. A place where I could feel that I was needed, I suppose.'

'Don't you feel that here?'

'No,' she replied, admitting the truth to herself. 'They've been very kind, but I don't really fit in. I've just felt as if I've been waiting for something to happen to take me away.'

'For your parents to find you, in other words.' She nodded silently and Morgan said, 'Well, now they have, so what's the point of staying here?'

'None, I suppose.' Lyn went to lean against the trunk of a tree. 'What did you mean when you said my father had asked you to take me back?'

'Exactly that. When he knew I was coming to Israel he asked me to find you, give you that letter, and take you back to England with me.'

'As simply as that! Didn't it occur to him that I might not want to go back?' she exclaimed indignantly.

'He's offering you his home, his love; what more can he do? You can't change the past, Lyn, you can only go forward. Do you want to be estranged from him indefinitely? The longer you leave it, the harder it's going to be to take that first step on the journey home, you know. If you're ever going to go back, then now is the time.'

She gave a shaky, somewhat defiant laugh. 'You're very persuasive on his behalf. Did he ask you to say all this?'

Morgan came swiftly to his feet in one easy movement and crossed to stand beside her, putting one hand on the tree trunk above her head. 'If I'm persuasive it's because I'd like you to see sense as soon as possible. I don't want to hang around here longer than necessary while you make up your mind,' he said tersely, in a change of mood that took her by surprise and made her feel vulnerable and unwanted.

She gave him a fiery look and moved away from the tree, feeling suddenly overwhelmed by his size and closeness. 'Then why don't you go? If I decide to go home I'm quite capable of making my own way there.

After all, I got here under my own steam,' she pointed out angrily.

'You father told me that after I'd found you I wasn't to let you out of my sight until I'd got you home. And that's just what I'm going to do.' Putting a firm hand on her arm, Morgan added, 'Let's go back to the village. I'm tired, even if you aren't.'

She resisted him for only a moment, but then fell into step beside him, walking along the path at the edge of the orchard. When they reached the kibbutz buildings she said, 'The guest house is over there.'

'I'll walk you back to your house.'

'No harm will come to me here,' she said in almost shocked protest.

'I'll walk you back, even so.'

His shadow, long and wide, travelled with her shorter one. Very few people, she felt, would want to tangle with a man like Morgan French, and Lyn felt an instinctive aura of security with him there. Not that she was about to let him see that. 'I really don't need an escort,' she said crossly, but then gave a gasp of fright as they neared her house and a dark shape moved on the veranda.

'It's OK, it's only me.' Dave came forward into the moonlight and looked at Morgan suspiciously. 'You OK?' he asked Lyn.

'Yes, fine. Goodnight.' Lyn nodded coolly to Morgan and walked into the house without introducing Dave.

She would have liked to go to her room to think things over in peace, but Dave had been good enough to wait up for her and deserved an explanation when he followed her in and asked who Morgan was. 'A friend of my father's,' she explained. 'He brought a letter for me.'

'What does he want?'

'My father? He wants me to go home.'

Dave halted for a moment, then said in a low voice so as not to wake the others, 'And will you go?'

'I don't know yet. I haven't made up my mind.' She gave a small smile. 'I'll sleep on it. Goodnight. See you tomorrow.'

But it was a long time before Lyn finally got to sleep. She lay wondering what to do, whether there would be any point in going back to England, or whether there was any point in staying here now. The only thing she *was* sure about was that she would never live in the same house as that woman her father had been stupid enough to marry. Maybe Morgan was right, she thought resignedly. Maybe it would be better to live on her own and to live a life completely independent of both her father and her mother. But it was hard, when you had been the only child of seemingly loving parents, to find that neither of them really wanted you any more.

Thinking of Morgan made her start to wonder about him again. He had been very autocratic in the way he'd said that he would take her back with him. Almost as if he wasn't giving her a choice. And he'd been very impatient with her when she couldn't make up her mind. Obviously he didn't really want to be bothered with her, either. But then, why should he? As far as he was concerned she was just another package that he'd promised to collect on his way back to England. From being the cherished child of doting parents, Lyn now felt completely unwanted. And it wasn't pleasant. She had naïvely thought that running away would make her parents united again in their worry over her, but it seemed to have had the opposite effect, and whatever she had sought in the kibbutz hadn't been there for her either. With a feeling of deep wretchedness, Lyn turned over and eventually fell asleep.

Morning lessons in the kibbutz school started early and Lyn only just made it in time. There were shadows round her eyes and she found it difficult to concentrate, the children taking advantage of her absent-mindedness during their English lesson until she belatedly called them to order. When she came out of school she half expected to see Morgan waiting for her and, strangely, felt disappointment, not relief, when he wasn't there. Having missed breakfast, Lyn went over to the dining-hall to get something to eat, but paused when she saw Morgan sitting outside under a shady umbrella, talking to Amos. For a moment she thought of hurrying away, but then her chin came up and she walked on, and was glad she had for they had obviously seen her. She nodded to them and gave them an over-bright, 'Good morning.'

Amos beckoned her over and she went reluctantly. 'I was just going to get myself something to eat.'

Morgan stood up. 'I'll get it. What do you want?'

'Coffee and a sandwich will do. Thank you.'

He left her with Amos, deliberately as it turned out, because Amos immediately told her that he thought it would be better if she left the kibbutz.

'But why?' Lyn protested. 'My work is OK, isn't

it?'

'This place isn't just to provide work, it's to give an opportunity of a different way of life. But our way isn't your way, Lyn. You know in your heart that's true.'

She looked down at her hands in her lap. 'Yes, I suppose so.'

'We've given you the breathing space you wanted,' Amos said firmly. 'And now it's time to go home and face your problems.'

'Did Morgan French make you tell me this?' Lyn demanded. 'He did, didn't he?'

He began, 'We are in agreement——'

But Lyn leaned forward angrily, saying, 'What right have either of you to decide my life for me?'

'None,' Amos agreed. 'Except that we are older and perhaps a little wiser, and you don't seem to know what it is you want to do.' He reached out and touched her hand. 'So go home, Lyn. You won't find any real happiness until you do.' Lyn was silent and he stood up. 'Come and say goodbye to me before you go.'

When Morgan came back with her food Lyn was sitting alone, staring down at the table and trying very hard not to cry. 'Coffee, and a cheese sandwich,' he told her. 'Hope that's OK?'

Unhappiness turned to anger and she glared at him as he sat down opposite her. 'You just don't care, do you?' she said bitterly. 'Just because you're in a hurry to be on your way, you have to get me kicked out of the kibbutz.' Morgan didn't deny it, but just watched her, his eyes narrowing. 'Couldn't you have waited a couple of days while I made up my mind?'

'To what purpose?' he said shortly. 'You're going

back to England with me and you know it.'

'No, I don't know it!' Lyn exclaimed, her voice rising as she got angrily to her feet.

But Morgan reached out and caught her wrist. 'Grow up, Lyn. This is no place for you. What's the point in hanging round to the bitter end? You know you're going to leave, so let's go.'

'I would have liked the privilege of making up my own mind,' she stormed, her grey eyes as cold as thunder-clouds.

He gave a short laugh. 'Privileges have to be earned.' Then, impatiently, 'Sit down and drink your coffee.'

Glancing round, Lyn saw that several people were looking at them and she reluctantly obeyed him. She felt angry but helpless. 'When do you want to leave?' she asked shortly.

'How long will it take you to pack?'

She stared at him, his words making her fully realise that her life here had come to an abrupt end. Turning away, she picked up her coffee-cup, but her hand was shaking and she had to use both to hold it steady. 'Are you always this—this despotic?' she asked unsteadily.

Morgan raised an eyebrow. 'Only when it's necessary.'

The note of mockery in his tone made Lyn decide that she disliked him intensely. Her hands tightened on the cup until her knuckles showed white, then abruptly she put it down and got to her feet. 'I'll be ready in an hour. I'll meet you outside the admin office.' And she strode away from him without a backward glance.

When the Rolls pulled up outside the office exactly an hour later, Lyn was ready and waiting. After one glance at her set face, Morgan didn't say anything until they were in the car and the kibbutz was left behind, but then he said, 'Congratulations. I know of very few women who could be packed and have her goodbyes said in an hour.' He gave a sideways look at her cold profile. 'I take it you did say goodbye?'

'Of course.' And her farewells had been met with good wishes, but Lyn knew that in a few days she would be forgotten; only Dave had insisted that she give him an address where he could write to her.

The Rolls bowled along at a steady but quite fast pace. Morgan took the coast road and Lyn stared out of the window, but not really seeing the scenery. It wasn't until they stopped at a garage to fill the tank that she roused herself enough to ask listlessly, 'Where are we heading?'

'To Haifa.' He waited for her to say something more, but when she relapsed into silence Morgan said shortly, 'I don't like sulky women, Lyn, so snap out of it.'

'I'm not sulking,' she retorted defensively. 'I'm—I'm sad.'

'What is there to be sad about? You're about to start a new phase of your life; you should be looking forward to it with optimism. You're going to see your father again, and then find somewhere to live and get a job, look up old frien——'

'Oh, for heaven's sake!' Lyn turned on him angrily. 'Just leave me alone, will you? I'll decide what I want to do when I get back to England. And I certainly don't need you to tell me. I don't know you and I don't want to know you. OK?'

Morgan gave her a grim look. 'Suit yourself.'

And so she would, Lyn decided firmly. She was fed up with being ordered around by Morgan and was glad that by tomorrow they would be in England and she wouldn't have to see him again. In the meantime she intended to ignore him.

So the rest of the journey to Haifa was a silent one, or would have been if Morgan hadn't turned on the radio and insisted on whistling along with the music. Lyn shot him a pointed look of annoyance, but he just grinned at her mockingly and went right on whistling until she could have screamed.

It was a relief to reach the port and drive to the wharf where a British ship was moored. Morgan went on board to see the captain and came back with several of the crew. He took their luggage from the car and Lyn stood on the dockside and watched as the Rolls was lifted by a huge crane and lashed on to the deck of the ship, Morgan anxiously superintending the operation. When it was done to his satisfaction he came down the gangway to her and picked up the cases. 'OK, let's go aboard.'

Lyn's eyes widened in amazement. 'But—but surely we're going to the airport to catch a plane?'

Morgan grinned at her, enjoying the moment. 'Sorry, but you and I are taking a very slow boat from Haifa. You didn't think I'd abandon the car, did you?' And he turned to climb the gangway again, taking Lyn's cases with him so that she had no choice but to follow him in stunned astonishment.

CHAPTER TWO

THE cargo ship the *British Bounty,* was almost new and surprisingly comfortable. A steward showed Lyn and Morgan to their cabins which were next door to each other on the starboard side. The cabins had portholes looking out to sea on one side and windows on to a secluded deck with a small pool on the other. Her cabin was bigger than Lyn had expected—in the little time she'd had to expect anything—and it was air-conditioned, too, which was welcome after standing on the hot quay. But Lyn gave little thought to the cabin; she was still too angry at the high-handed way in which Morgan had announced that they were travelling on the ship.

The steward showed her how to use the shower and, after he'd gone, Lyn made full use of it, the water cooling her heated body but not her anger. By the time she had dried herself and dressed, the sun was very low in the sky, turning the water in the harbour to a deep gold. There were lots of other ships in the port, some of them still being loaded with the huge containers that she had seen waiting on the dock as they drove past.

At seven-thirty the steward came to show her the way to the dining-room and passenger lounge. Morgan was already there, talking to a man in uniform and leaning against a small bar. He straightened up when Lyn came into the room and looked at her quizzically, his mouth quirking when a fiery glance from her grey eyes told him that she was still mad at him. 'This is Browning, the second mate,' he told her, indicating the man at his side. 'Lyn Standish.'

'*Tim* Browning,' the man offered. He was quite young, with dark curly hair, his complexion burnt to mahogany by the sun.

'What would you like to drink?' Morgan asked her.

'A double vodka and tonic,' she answered on a challenging note. But rather to her disappointment Morgan merely turned to the bar steward and ordered it.

Some more people came in: two middle-aged married couples, the captain, two Israeli students, two more officers, and a pair of elderly ladies who looked so alike that they had to be sisters. Tim Browning moved away to welcome them and Lyn said to Morgan, 'I'm surprised you were able to get me a berth on the ship at the last minute; it looks pretty full.'

'What makes you think it was a last-minute reservation?'

'Well, we only arrived on the quay a few hours ago. I. . .' Her voice died as she saw the look in his blue eyes. 'But you had already made the reservation, hadn't you?' she said accusingly. Adding bitterly, 'You must have been very sure that I'd come with you.'

'If you hadn't, I would have kidnapped you,' Morgan said lightly.

He grinned at her, but Lyn wasn't to be appeased so easily. She glared at him and was about to say something cutting, but one of the ship's officers came over with the rest of the passengers in tow.

Introductions were made but Lyn didn't really take in any of the names. She took the drink that Morgan offered her and walked over to Tim Browning. 'How long will it take for the boat to get to England?'

'About a month,' he answered cheerfully.

'A month!' Lyn stared at him in consternation. 'But surely it isn't that far?'

'No, but we have several ports of call on the way,' Tim explained.

'Told you it was a very slow boat,' Morgan murmured in her ear.

She swung round on him, eyes flashing angrily. 'We could have taken a plane and been in London by tomorrow.'

'I know.'

'So why spend weeks stuck on this tub?'

'Tut tut,' Morgan reprimanded. 'Better not let the master hear you calling it that or he might clap you in irons.'

'Oh, for heaven's sake!' she said furiously. 'It isn't funny.'

'Nor is it worth getting so worked up about,' Morgan pointed out, his voice hardening. 'You were in no hurry to get home, so what difference does it make if you spend a few weeks getting there?'

'The difference is,' she said in a fierce undertone, 'that the few weeks will have to be spent in *your* company.'

Morgan's left eyebrow rose. 'Anyone would think you didn't like me.'

'And anyone would be *right!*'

He gave her a mock woeful look but his eyes were

amused. 'I'm devastated.'

Lyn opened her mouth to make a sharp retort but
then bit her lip, knowing that her anger meant nothing
to him. He expected her to fall in with his plans, and
if she didn't like it that was just too bad. She turned
and lifted her drink to her mouth, trying to appear calm
but inwardly seething at his high-handedness. She
wasn't used to being used like this; before her parents'
marriage had broken up she had always had her
preferences deferred to, and even in the kibbutz she
had been treated with more respect. One of the elderly
sisters started talking to Morgan, so Lyn took the
opportunity to move nearer to Tim Browning.

'When does the boat sail?' she asked him in a low
voice, hoping that Morgan wouldn't overhear.

'Not till the early hours of the morning, when you'll
still be fast asleep,' he told her cheerfully.

A steward announced dinner a few moments later.
There was just one long table in the dining-saloon and
Lyn took good care not to sit next to Morgan, instead
finding a place next to one of the Israeli students. They
managed to converse a little in a mixture of English
and Hebrew and she learned that they were only
travelling as far as the first port of call, Alexandria.
After dinner the officers went back to work and the
passengers went into the next-door lounge where the
bar was. Being a small group, they were already
beginning to socialise, but Lyn merely said goodnight
to the student and went to her cabin. There she changed
into jeans and a blouse and packed a few things into a
holdall, then lay on the bed, setting her travel alarm
clock for one in the morning, just in case she fell

asleep.

But too much had happened today and she was too mad to sleep. She read her father's letter through a couple of times more, still hardly able to believe that her mother had married again. And without telling her or trying to find her. That hurt, it really did.

She lay and listened to the unusual noises; the metallic echoes of the boat, the throbbing engines of other ships in the harbour, and the constant vibration of the cranes on the dock, forever busy loading and unloading. The groans of a watery hell, she thought, remembering the tranquillity of the kibbutz, and wondering if any of its produce was even now being loaded into the deep hold of a nearby ship.

The sounds on board the *British Bounty* lessened, and at one o'clock Lyn got up, put on a jacket, and picked up her holdall. Opening the door a little, she peeped out and saw that there was no one around. Quietly she made her way down to the main deck and saw to her relief that the gangway was still in place. There was an officer at its head, but after a few minutes someone called him and she was able to slip down it while his back was turned and run quickly across the lit quay into a dark patch of shadow. For a few anxious minutes she waited in case anyone had spotted her, but the ship was quiet. With a gleeful chuckle at the ease of her escape, Lyn shouldered the holdall and strode rapidly through the dock in the direction of the town.

There were guards at the entrance to the dock but they took no notice of someone leaving. Lyn had never been to Haifa before and didn't know the layout of the town, but was confident that if she walked towards its centre she would eventually find a taxi which would take her to the nearest airport. Her only worry was that she might not have enough shekels to pay for the ride. The buildings on either side seemed to be mostly warehouses, the majority of which were in darkness. There were very few ordinary houses and no people around. She began to be conscious of the tall buildings and the emptiness pressing in on her as her footsteps echoed along the road. A sound seemed to come from behind her and she swung round nervously, but she couldn't see anyone. Her pace quickening, Lyn hurried along, and gave a sigh of relief when she saw the lights of a café further down the street. Great! Now she could phone for a taxi.

But when Lyn pushed open the door and went into the brightly lit, smoke-heavy atmosphere she found to her consternation that the place was more of a bar than a café. There were several customers, all men, dressed in the rough working clothes of sailors, whose conversation immediately stopped when she walked in. She felt their eyes on her, looking her over assessingly, and knew at once that it had been a mistake to come in here. But it was too late now. Ignoring the stares of the men, she went up to the beer-stained counter where the proprietor leaned, a tattooed snake writhing up his arm. 'Please, do you speak English?'

His eyes went over her again. 'Perhaps.'

'May I use your telephone to call a taxi?'

He gave her an unpleasant smile. 'No phone.'

'But you must have!' Lyn exclaimed in alarm.

But he merely shrugged so that the snake moved

like a live thing. Unused to such rudeness, Lyn turned and went out into the street again, but was dismayed to hear someone come out behind her. She didn't turn round but there were definitely footsteps following her now, and within a short distance two of the men from the bar caught her up, moving one on either side of her.

'We show you where is telephone,' the man on her left said, putting a hand on her arm.

She stood still, looking at them. They were both short, dark, and had swarthy complexions. They could have come from any Middle Eastern country, and the word 'Lascar' leapt into her mind. 'Thanks, but I've changed my mind,' she said shortly, and turning round began to hurry back towards the docks.

But the sailor who had taken her arm wouldn't let go, and the other man caught hold of her as well when she tried to struggle. Suddenly they began to run with her, pulling her almost off her feet and dragging her, kicking and struggling, into the entrance to an alleyway, then pushed her up against the wall. 'No!' Lyn cried out in terror as their hands went to her clothes.

One man laughed in her face, his vile breath making her cringe away, but suddenly his laughter was bitten off and he began to choke and gasp as his sweater was twisted into a tight knot at the back of his neck. Her startled eyes probing the darkness, Lyn looked past him and gave a great sob of thankfulness. 'Morgan!'

The second sailor turned to see what had happened and Lyn was able to wrench herself free and run out into the street. There was the sound of a scuffle behind her but it was only a few minutes before Morgan came out of the alleyway, brushing down his jacket. He didn't say anything, just picked up her holdall from where she'd dropped it and, taking her arm, marched her grimly past the bar and back towards the docks. He took such long strides that Lyn had to almost run to keep up with him. She kept looking back over her shoulder, afraid that the two sailors might come after them, and as eager now to get back to the ship as she had been to leave it.

The engines were running and there were signs that the ship was about to sail when Morgan pushed her ahead of him up the gangway. The duty officer grinned at them. 'Been for a last walk on dry land?'

'Something like that,' Morgan agreed. His grip tightening, he led Lyn into the empty passenger lounge and shut the door firmly behind him. 'And just where do you think you were going?' he demanded menacingly, his hands on his hips as he glared at her.

'Thank goodness you came along,' Lyn gasped, trying to divert him. 'I was so afraid. But you were magnificent! So brave, the way you dealt with them. I bet they don't——'

'Stop trying to flatter me,' Morgan broke in rudely, 'because it isn't going to work. You were clearing out —and without saying a word!'

'I'm trying to thank you,' Lyn persisted.

'OK, so you've thanked me. Do you realise what an abysmally stupid thing you did?' Morgan exclaimed shortly. 'Didn't it once occur to you than an eastern port in the early hours of the morning might be dangerous? What are you—some kind of nut, or just a stupid idiot?'

Her cheeks flushed, Lyn said unsteadily, 'I just wanted to go home by plane, that's all. How was I to know that those men would—would. . .'

'Because you're a beautiful young girl, of course! What the hell did you expect,' Morgan retorted angrily. 'Just count yourself darn lucky that I happened to find out that you were gone, that's all. I——' His next words were drowned beneath the sound of the ship's siren as the mooring lines were let go and the harbour tugs turned her towards the open sea.

They stood silently, listening, until the noise had died down a little then Lyn said in a brittle, defiant voice, 'OK, I'm sorry.'

Morgan's reply was brusque. 'White slavery may be uncommon nowadays but it hasn't died out completely, you know. You were taking a hell of a risk, Lyn.' She averted her face, remembering the sailors' faces and their hands touching her, but Morgan mistook her action and said harshly, 'I suppose you're planning to try this again when we reach Alexandria? Well, you can put the idea out of your head, because you're going all the way to England on this ship even if I have to lock you in your cabin at every port we stop at.'

'You wouldn't dare!' Lyn exclaimed, shocked.

He stuck his chin out belligerently. 'Oh, wouldn't I?'

He would, too, she realised, staring up at him in wide-eyed apprehension. She had thought Morgan to have a strong character the first time she'd met him, but usually he kept it hidden behind an air of casualness. Tonight he'd shown just how tough he really was. And strangely there had been no doubt in her mind back there in the alleyway that he was quite capable of handling two vicious characters who had probably been in a dozen knife fights before.

The thought of him being stabbed made her tremble suddenly and she said in a small voice, 'I haven't asked you if you were hurt.'

'No, I wasn't. Thanks,' he added.

'There's a tear in your jacket.' She moved to stand beside him and lifted her finger to run the tip along the cut in his sleeve.

Morgan twisted his head round to look. 'It could have happened at any time,' he said dismissively.

But she knew that it had happened tonight. 'I'm sorry,' she said again, meaning it this time.

Putting his hand under her chin, Morgan lifted her face and looked at her intently. 'Does that mean that you'll promise not to try and run away again?'

She gave him a puzzled look. 'I just don't understand why you want me to go by sea. Are you afraid that I won't go back to England?'

'Perhaps.'

'But I've said that I'll go home. You can even put me on a plane if you don't believe me.'

His blue eyes narrowed a little. 'Maybe I don't want to put you on a plane. Maybe I want to keep you here with me.'

Disconcerted, Lyn's eyes widened and she tried to read his expression, but he immediately let her go and straightened up. 'It's late,' he said on a curt note. 'I'm going to turn in. Are you coming?'

He held the door open for her and she preceded him down the passageway to the passenger quarters. She wondered whether he would check to make sure that she went in, but he merely nodded, 'Goodnight,' and went into his own cabin.

So she was back! Lyn looked ruefully round the cabin but was more than glad to be there safely. She showered away the touch of the sailors' hands from her skin, the memory of their faces from her mind, and gave a prayer of thankfulness for sending Morgan to save her. But it wasn't until Lyn was lying in her bed, and trying to adjust to the motion of the ship, that it occurred to her that the only way Morgan could have known she wasn't on the ship was by going to her cabin himself!

She woke next morning to the sound of voices and peeked out of her cabin window to see several of the passengers taking breakfast in the sun on the deck outside. The sight of food made her feel hungry and she soon joined the others, although Morgan wasn't among them. Her curiosity got the better of her after she'd eaten and she strolled round the ship, wondering where he could be, eventually finding him working out in the ship's small gymnasium with Tim Browning. The gym had a glass door and she watched the two men through it. Both were wearing only sports vests and shorts and were of a similar height, but Morgan's body was far more athletic and muscular, obviously in the peak of condition as he did pull-ups, his hands clasped behind his head, his tight stomach muscles easily taking the strain. He looked so fit and tanned that it occurred to her to wonder what he did for a living. He certainly didn't look as if he was tied to an office desk all day, or the deck of a ship as Tim was.

Coming to the end of their exercise, the two men stood up and Lyn moved quickly away, not wanting to be thought of as a female voyeur.

When Morgan came back to the passenger deck Lyn was stretched out on a sun-lounger in a white one-piece swimsuit, the two students in close attendance. He came over to her and the two younger men quickly got up and excused themselves, intimidated by his air of slightly sardonic authority. Hooking up a lounger, Morgan signalled to the waiter and sat down beside her. 'How are you this morning?'

'Fine, thanks.'

'But still angry that you're here on the ship, I take it?'

'Shouldn't I be?'

'Just accept it, Lyn—you're here to stay.' She turned to look at him, her gaze more curious than antagonistic, and he raised an eyebrow. 'Now what are you thinking, I wonder?'

'Just that two days ago I'd never even met you and now you seem to have taken over my life.'

'And I suppose you resent that, too.' The waiter came up and he ordered two coffees without consulting her.

'Anyone would resent having their life taken over. And I like to be asked what I want to drink,' Lyn added tartly.

'Don't you want a coffee?'

'That's not the point. The point is that you should

have *asked* me.'

Morgan smiled and, leaning back in the chair, closed his eyes. Angrily Lyn poked him in the ribs. 'Ouch! What was that for?' he asked.

'Because you're not listening to me.'

'On the contrary, I heard every word.'

'Well, you're not taking any notice, then. I don't like being taken for granted,' Lyn said forcefully.

He looked at her mutinous face for a moment, and then deliberately let his eyes travel slowly and appreciatively down the length of her slim figure in the clinging white swimsuit and back to her face. Softly he said, 'You don't have to worry, Lyn—I shall *never* take you for granted.'

She gazed into his face for a moment and then turned away, staring unseeingly down the deck. This habit he had, of treating her one moment as a schoolgirl and then as an attractive woman, had disconcerted her yet again. Her heart was beating a little fast and she felt a warm glow of awareness. And the way he had said it, as if he meant their relationship to go on into the future, that brought all sorts of possibilities to her mind too.

The waiter brought their coffee and they were joined by one of the married couples. This was the disadvantage of such a small ship, Lyn found during the next few days; apart from her own cabin there was nowhere she could go to avoid the other passengers. And because there were so few of them they all took it as their right or duty to fall into conversation whenever they saw her alone. Even lying on a sun lounger with her eyes tightly closed didn't stop them.

And some of them were so nosy! Lyn got tired of fielding subtle—or sometimes very direct—questions about her relationship with Morgan. Questions she couldn't answer because she had no very clear idea herself.

They had been thrown together in such a strange way. If they had taken a plane to England she would have said goodbye to Morgan at Heathrow Airport and probably never seen him again, but, faced with being in his close company for a month, Lyn found that she had to get to know him better whether she wanted to or not. And, strangely, she realised that she did want to.

Although he had joined her on that first morning, Morgan by no means hung around her. He was a very active person, willing to play deck tennis with anyone who asked him, and spending a lot of time swimming in the pool or giving diving lessons to the two students. That was when he wasn't working out in the gym or jogging round the deck with one or other of the officers, of course. And in the evenings he mingled with the other passengers in well-mannered politeness, playing bridge or taking part in whatever entertainment happened to be suggested, although Lyn noticed that he managed to quietly disappear if the games became too juvenile, like clock golf or Trivial Pursuit.

On their third evening on the ship, Lyn noticed that he was no longer in the passenger lounge and went down to the main deck to look for him. It was a very clear night with a bright moon but there was quite a strong breeze from the sea. She was wearing a dress of turquoise Indian cotton, her tanned skin showing through the sleeves. Pausing at the rail, Lyn tilted her face to the wind, closing her eyes as she put her hands behind her head to lift her hair and let it cool her face and neck, the thin material of the dress blown against her to mould the outline of her slim body. Behind her she heard the soft sounds of unhurried footsteps, but before she could turn round there was a sharp intake of breath and the footsteps came to a sudden stop. Turning, she saw that Morgan had come round the corner of the deck and was standing a few feet away, but he had his back to the moon and she couldn't see his face.

For a long moment neither of them spoke, but then Morgan shoved his hands into his pockets and sauntered over to stand beside her and lean against the rail. 'Get fed up with playing Monopoly?' he said casually.

'Mm.' She leaned alongside him. 'Do you think they'll want to play games every night?'

'Bound to. It's *de rigueur* on a cruise.'

'It's childish.'

Morgan chuckled and for a moment she thought he was going to make some comment about her still being a child, but he only said, 'That's half the fun of being on holiday.'

'What have *you* been doing?'

'Checking on the Rolls.'

'You really worry about that car,' Lyn commented, her voice having an unknowingly jealous note. 'I bet you wish you could keep it.'

'That's not practical, I'm afraid. I haven't anywhere

to garage it.'

'Don't you have a house?'

'No, only a flat with on-street parking.'

'Where? In London?'

'Yes. Kensington.'

'And what do you do—when you're not collecting cars and wayward daughters?' Lyn asked on a wry note.

Grinning, Morgan turned to lean back against the rail so that he could look at her. '"Wayward daughters"—I like that.' Lifting his hand he ran the back of his finger down her cheek. 'And do I have to lock you in your cabin when we reach Alexandria tomorrow?'

A tremor ran through her and she straightened up, her hands gripping the cool metal of the rail, completely forgetting that he hadn't answered her question. Her stomach felt churny inside and her throat was tight. Suddenly she knew that leaving the ship, leaving Morgan, was the last thing she wanted to do. But there was no way she was going to let him know that, of course. 'How long will we be in port?' she temporised.

'Two or three days,' he answered, his eyes fixed on her face.

'And do you intend to keep me a prisoner on board all that time?'

'If I have to. I certainly don't intend to keep chasing to the airport after you,' he added firmly.

Lyn smiled. 'There isn't an international airport at Alexandria.'

'So?'

She shrugged and half turned towards him. 'So I give you my word I won't try to run away—while we're in Alexandria,' she couldn't resist adding on a teasing note.

'Good.' Morgan straightened up and put one hand on her arm, and with the other tilted her chin. Lyn's heart seemed to stop as she realised that he was going to kiss her. She had time to push him away, to tell him to let her go, but she did neither of those things. Instead she just stood there, her feelings overcome by his closeness and the sheer maleness of him. He bent his head—just as someone cleared their throat loudly nearby. Morgan paused, and instead of kissing her his lips merely brushed her cheek. 'Goodnight, Lyn.'

'Goodnight.' Her thoughts a whirl of disappointment, she turned to go in and saw one of the male passengers gazing out to sea and trying to appear as if he wasn't watching them. She said a stiff goodnight to him and went up to the passenger deck, wondering if Morgan would have really kissed her if the wretched man hadn't come along.

When she woke the next morning they were tied up in Alexandria harbour. It was very noisy and smelly after the peace of the open sea, but the bustle and activity of the port was an interesting sight after nothing but the ship and the horizon. Lyn had never been to Alexandria before and wondered if Morgan would let her go ashore. That thought pulled her up short; he wasn't her keeper, even if he liked to think he was. For a brief second she felt a flash of indignation, but then grinned to herself; Morgan had a thing or two to learn about the emancipation of women, and teaching him just might be quite pleasant.

The two Israeli students were leaving the ship here, but not until the next day when they were due to board another ship that would take them on to America. So that night turned into a sort of farewell party for them with all the passengers and a couple of the ship's officers going ashore to a nightclub. It was a far livelier place than any club Lyn had ever been to in England. The music was eastern; played by sweating men on unfamiliar instruments, it jangled unharmoniously in Lyn's ears. The place was crowded, too, and they all had to squeeze round a table that was too small. None of the customers seemed to take any notice of the band, instead talking volubly and loudly, so that the place was full of noise. Lyn, squashed between Morgan and one of the students, looked round the place and loved it.

'You OK?' Morgan asked in her ear.

She grinned at him and nodded enthusiastically. 'Yes, great. Can I have one of those?' she asked, pointing to a neighbouring table where a waiter had brought some lurid-coloured cocktails.

'Good grief!' But Morgan ordered the drink, although he stuck to whisky himself, and watched, fascinated, as she took the first sip. 'What's it like?'

'Not bad.' Actually Lyn was rather disappointed; it was more innocuous than she had imagined and tasted rather sweet.

The room was very hot with so many people there. They had several more drinks and had to raise their voices above the noise, the room only becoming quiet when the cabaret came on. First there was a female singer who sang western songs, and after that three belly-dancers. It wasn't a form of entertainment that Lyn went for very much, but the men in the room, and there were far more men than women, all seemed to love it. One dancer, her hair hanging to her waist and dressed in a spangled pink outfit—what there was of it—came over to the corner of the dance floor nearest to their table and writhed and shook before them, her sinuous figure throbbing to the beat of the music.

Lyn sat back, watching the faces of the people around her. The women's expressions were a picture: half disapproving but with a trace of fascinated envy deep in their eyes. The two middle-aged men and the students were clapping enthusiastically, but the sailors had seen it all before and appeared to be more blasé, although Lyn noticed that their features were sharpened by the eroticism of the dance. Her eyes flicked to Morgan. He was leaning back in his seat, watching the dancer, an amused twist to his mouth but no cupidity in his face. Feeling her watching him, he turned his head and met her gaze—and seemed to know immediately what she was thinking. His smile deepened and he reached out to take her hand. For a few moments he played with her fingers teasingly, but then lifted her hand to his mouth and turned it over to lightly kiss her palm, his mocking blue eyes holding hers the while.

Lyn's heart gave a crazy kind of lurch and for a moment her fingers curled over his, but then she blinked and went to take her hand away—only Morgan wouldn't let her. She stared at him and felt suddenly as if they were alone in that crowded place, as if the beat of the music was the beat of her heart, the heat the fire in her own blood, the noise of clapping the crazy clamour of her own whirling brain. Time seemed to stand still as the mockery left Morgan's face and his features grew tense as he gazed at her. His fingers tightened convulsively on her hand, hurting her, but she hardly noticed the pain. The music came to a jangling, strident halt and Morgan suddenly let go of her hand and turned away to join in the applause, an almost stunned look in his eyes.

Her breathing unsteady, Lyn, too, turned to face the dance floor and to clap enthusiastically. She couldn't think why she hadn't liked the music before; it was the best she'd ever heard.

It was very late when they left the club and crowded into two taxis to go back to the ship. Lyn found herself sitting on Morgan's lap in the back of one and wasn't at all sure how she got there. But she was happy being there. Definitely. She could feel his arm round her, warm and strong as he supported her, and the hardness of his thighs beneath her. She sat up straight at first but her head was against the roof, so it seemed quite natural to lean back against him and put her head on his shoulder.

'Minx,' he breathed in her ear.

She chuckled and moved into a more comfortable position, making him catch his breath. His arms tightened and she felt a glorious feeling of power at this evidence that he wasn't immune to her. The faintly musky smell of his skin filled her nostrils, arousing a primitive, sensuous desire that made her feel empty deep inside. She wanted to put her arms round his neck and have him kiss her, to be held against his hard body and have him satisfy this need that grew with every passing moment. But there were four other people squeezed into the taxi: the two ship's officers and the spinster sisters, one of whom was seated on Tim Browning's knee beside them and thoroughly enjoying herself, giggling away like a young girl. Lyn almost felt old beside her.

They reached the dock far too soon and Lyn's legs felt strangely wobbly when she got out. Maybe those drinks had been more powerful than she thought. Morgan put his arm round her when she staggered a little. 'Steady.' He helped her up the gangway and to the passenger deck. 'You'd better go to bed.'

'No, I don't want to.' Lyn broke from his hold but caught his hand. 'Let's go and count the stars,' she said on a high, excited note, trying to pull him with her.

He allowed her to lead him forward to the bow of the ship, but his steps were far from eager. It was sheltered here, the sides glassed in to keep out the wind and make a sun-trap for the passengers to relax on the loungers that were stacked against the wall. There was a light, too, but Lyn reached up and turned it off, letting the moon take over. She turned to Morgan and put her hands on his shoulders, her head raised for his kiss, her mouth parted sensuously. He lifted his hands to cover hers and gazed down at her, his eyes glittering in the moonlight, but he didn't bend to kiss her.

Impatiently Lyn reached up and put a hand behind his neck, then stood on tiptoe to kiss him. For a moment their lips met and she felt the hardness of his mouth. Her eyes closed and she moved against him, letting herself drown in the heady, overwhelming sensuality of his nearness. But then Morgan stepped back abruptly, almost pushing her from him.

Opening her eyes, Lyn stared at him in bewilderment. 'What is it? What's the matter?'

His voice harsh, Morgan said, 'Go to bed, Lyn. You don't know what you're doing.'

She straightened indignantly but had to grab hold of the rail as she felt suddenly giddy. 'Are you saying I'm too young?' she demanded hotly.

'I'm saying you've had too much to drink—and I don't take advantage of girls in your state,' Morgan retorted.

'I am *not* drunk,' Lyn flashed back, her hand holding tightly to the rail. 'And I'm not exactly inexperienced, either,' she added triumphantly.

'Really?' Morgan's voice was wry. Putting his hand on her arm, he glared down at her, his face angry now. 'Well, maybe I'll find out whether that's true or not some time, but understand this, Lyn: when I want a girl, then I make the running. OK?'

She stared up at him, feeling suddenly sober—and very much out of her depth. The seriousness in his face disconcerted her so that she gulped and nodded. But then suddenly his mood changed and Morgan grinned, his old self again. 'Come on, I'll help you back to your cabin. I'm afraid you're going to have a hell of a hangover in the morning.'

But, strangely, when Lyn woke the next day she felt fine. She had slept late though and was only just in time to say goodbye to the students, who really looked the worse for wear. Morgan gave her a disbelieving look. 'Haven't you even got a headache? I was sure you'd be out for the rest of the day.'

'Perhaps I wasn't as tight as you thought,' Lyn countered, looking at him with a slight flush to her cheeks as she remembered last night.

His eyes went swiftly to her face and he frowned, then turned away to wave to the students as they walked down the dock. He left her then to play deck tennis until lunch, and afterwards they all went on a guided tour round the town, but Morgan paid hardly more attention to her than he did to the other women in the party. At first his attitude humiliated and angered her, but then she happened to catch his eye once and he winked at her. She felt confused, until she realised that they would be spending the next few weeks in the company of the other passengers and there would be little privacy on the ship. It was no place for a romance to develop. And she *had* been a little tipsy last night, so really she ought to be grateful that he hadn't taken it further. Not that she felt in the least grateful. But she was intrigued by his statement that *he* would make the running. Would he? she wondered. And if so, when? Lyn watched him as he stood tall in the sun and, her heart thudding in anticipation, hoped that he would make it soon.

CHAPTER THREE

THE Mediterranean sun beat down on the deck of the ship as the *British Bounty* made its unhurried way from port to port. From Alexandria it sailed to Benghazi to pick up more cargo, and then on to Tripoli where it unloaded produce from Israel. In Tripoli it also picked up two more passengers: another middle-aged married couple, French this time. Their arrival was greeted with pleasure all round because they turned out to be good bridge players, and so were able to make up another four with the spinster sisters in the almost nightly game. When Lyn had been asked to make up a bridge table she hadn't played well, finding it difficult to concentrate, especially when Morgan was her partner, so it was a relief to them all when the new people came on board. And this, of course, left Lyn and Morgan free to amuse themselves.

It was an unhurried life, and Lyn found that she had to adjust herself to the pace—or lack of it. Even in the kibbutz there had been work to do, and her life had been governed by time so that there had been a sense of urgency, but on the ship she only had to roll up for meals—and not then if she didn't feel like eating. She grew sleek and brown from swimming in the pool and sunbathing, her body glowed with health and her fair hair fell in a tumbling mass of molten gold on her tanned shoulders.

She spent a lot of time with Morgan, although they

were seldom completely alone. Lyn didn't mind that as much as she had thought she would, perhaps because the voyage was going to take so long and the weeks stretched ahead of them. *Mañana* could be very seductive, very catching, a languorous luxury of time when you had nothing to dwell on but your own self and your own feelings. They talked a lot, relaxing on loungers by the pool or under the shade of an umbrella in the hottest part of the day. At first they discussed impartial things, but Lyn gradually began to confide in Morgan, for the first time putting into words her feelings about her parents' marriage break-up. The hatred towards her new stepmother was still there, and very strong, although Morgan tried to dispel it. That he should do so surprised Lyn and she told him so.

'What's the point in going on hating her?' Morgan replied casually. 'Your parents have divorced and married again; if your mother can forget enough to start a new life, why can't you?'

'I don't believe she has forgotten, and I'm sure she hasn't forgiven *that woman* for what she did,' Lyn answered with certainty.

'Her name's Claire, isn't it? Why don't you call her by her name instead of "that woman"?' Morgan said on a strangely irritable note. He caught the surprised look in Lyn's eyes, and added, 'You're too young to be so dogmatic.' He was silent for a moment, then went on, 'Going on hating her isn't good for you, Lyn. Think about it; if you love your father and want to be part of his life, then you'll just have to learn to accept his wife. You do *want* to be part of his life, don't you?'

Sitting up on the lounger, Lyn raised her knees and

propped her chin on them. 'Do I want to be part of his life—or do I want him to be part of mine?'

'Is there a difference?'

'I think so. I don't want to be part of his life if it means being nice to that wo— to Claire, but he could be part of *my* life if we saw each other without her.'

'That's childish and petty,' Morgan said brusquely.

Lyn's chin came up. 'You always say that if I don't agree with your opinion,' she retorted.

Morgan grinned and reached out to draw a lazy finger down her bare spine, from her neck, over the strap of her bikini top and on down. 'But you know that I'm right,' he insisted.

A tremor ran through her and her throat felt tight. When he touched her like that, even though he did it so casually, it did crazy things to her senses. They hadn't kissed yet, not properly, and Morgan betrayed no possessiveness or urgency, but Lyn knew with deep feminine awareness that he would. Some time soon, before the voyage was over.

In the late afternoon on their second day out from Tripoli, Morgan and Lyn had been playing a vigorous game of deck tennis and went to their cabins early to shower and change for dinner. A thrill of excited anticipation ran through her as Lyn dressed. Tonight there would be no game of bridge; they would be able to leave the others in the lounge and be on their own. She paused in only her underwear to look in the long mirror, seeing the reflection of her figure, still very slim and boyish, her stomach flat and her breasts firm and tilted, her skin with the velvet elasticity of youth. Did Morgan fancy her? she wondered, but knew that he did. His eyes had betrayed his feelings even if he had never said it. He had never told her, either, whether he had a girlfriend, and she had been afraid to ask. But she hadn't needed to ask if he was experienced with women; that showed in his complete self-assurance, in his charm when he was with the other women passengers, and in his slight air of mockery when he looked at Lyn. But perhaps the mockery was aimed at himself.

It was too hot for a bra, even the wispy piece of lace that Lyn was wearing. She took it off and chose a sun-top and matching skirt that she had bought from a market in Tripoli. The material was blue and had reminded her of the colour of Morgan's eyes. Brushing her hair she tied it up off her face, leaving just curling wisps at the sides. She was so tanned that she needed little make-up, just lipstick, and mascara to darken her long eyelashes. And perfume, of course. Lyn applied that with a more liberal hand. When she was ready she took another critical look at herself in the mirror. Yes, she would do—hopefully. She caught a look of sensuous anticipation in her face and was surprised that her feelings were so transparent.

The look was still there when she left her cabin a few minutes later—and bumped straight into Morgan leaving his!

'Sorry.' His hand came up to steady her. He looked at her and grew still for a moment, an arrested expression in his face. Then he dragged his eyes away to glance over her head. 'You look very lovely tonight,' he said on a slightly unsteady note.

'Thanks. So—so do you,' Lyn said breathlessly.

Immediately his mood changed and he laughed in amusement. 'I'm not sure whether I ought to thank you for that or not.'

She flushed, feeling gauche and angry with herself. 'You know what I mean.'

'Yes. And thanks.' His eyes, still creased with laughter, lingered on her face, but then he gave a quick frown and looked away.

They didn't sit next to each other during the meal, but afterwards Morgan suggested having a drink outside. Lyn felt speculative eyes watching her as she left the lounge; among the other passengers and the crew they were looked on as a couple, even though they had separate cabins. Lyn had an idea that bets were now being taken as to their relationship, but there was no way she was going to admit to the frequent questioners that Morgan was her—what? She would have said gaoler once, but not now; she hadn't even bothered to make any more promises about not running away since Alexandria because they both knew that she wouldn't. So what did that make Morgan? Her guardian, *in loco parentis*? That thought made her smile; there was nothing at all parental or even avuncular about his attitude to her, even though he was over ten years older.

'What are you thinking?' Morgan asked curiously, as he came over with her drink to where she was sitting out on the cool of the deck.

'About you,' she answered frankly.

He gave her a non-committal look. 'Can't you find anything more interesting to think about?'

'Maybe I do find you interesting,' she countered.

He grinned and sat down beside her. 'Somehow I think that ought to be my line.'

Ignoring that, Lyn said, 'Although I really don't know very much about you, do I? You encourage me to talk to you about myself, but you hardly ever talk about you.'

'There's little to tell,' he said dismissively.

'I don't believe that. You haven't even told me what you do for a living.'

'Not a lot,' he answered offhandedly. 'A deal here, picking up a car there.'

'Don't you have a career?' Lyn asked on a surprised note, conditioned from childhood to think that all men should have a profession.

'A career?' His mouth twisted sardonically. 'Careers don't always turn out to be what you expect them to be.'

That sounded intriguing. She looked at him more closely, but Morgan was good at hiding his feelings and she had to say directly, 'What do you mean?'

'Nothing much.' Turning his head, he said, 'You think having some kind of a profession is important, do you?'

'Well, how else can you earn a living?'

'So what's your profession?' he asked bluntly. 'Waitressing?'

Lyn was taken aback. 'No, of course not. That was only a job I was given to do while I was in the kibbutz. You can't call being a waitress a career.'

'Why not? Any job if it's done in a professional manner becomes a career; doesn't matter what it is,' he said with conviction. 'So what do you do, then?'

'Well, I did office work for a few months.' Lyn

looked up to find his blue eyes were fixed steadily on her face and flushed. 'OK, so it was in one of Daddy's companies when one of the girls was away on maternity leave. I haven't done much else, but Daddy always said there was no need for me to work, that I should enjoy myself while I was young.'

'You sound like a spoilt brat,' Morgan remarked, leaning back to close his eyes as if he found her thoroughly boring.

She stared at his reclining figure indignantly, realising that he'd changed the subject from himself yet again. A wicked gleam came into her eyes and Lyn got quietly to her feet. Going into the bar she helped herself to a handful of ice chips from the bucket, then calmly walked up behind Morgan, pulled back his shirt collar and thrust the ice down his back before he knew what was happening.

He let out a yell and shot to his feet, but Lyn didn't hang around. She took off down the deck, leaping the companionway half a dozen steps at a time and dodging round the deck cargo as she heard his steps thudding after her. A couple of the crew who were on watch began to cheer and whistle, but whether they were encouraging her or Morgan, Lyn didn't know. By now she was fully familiar with the layout of the ship and could take advantage of the shadows to elude him and the various companionways to go from deck to deck. She might even have got away from him altogether if he hadn't cleverly anticipated which way she would go and jumped out of a doorway just as she ran past.

Lyn gave a cry of delicious fright as Morgan

grabbed her, his arms going round her in a bear-hug—a bear with limbs of steel. 'Put ice down my neck, would you?' he growled at her, his teeth drawn back in a menacing grin that promised retribution.

'It was your own fault,' she retorted on a high note that was half laughing, half fascinated fear, as she tried in vain to break free. 'You were darn rude to me.'

But he took no notice, instead saying, 'Little girls who play tricks on people deserve to be punished.' And with a quick movement he picked her up in his arms and began to carry her back towards the passenger deck.

'What are you going to do?' Lyn demanded apprehensively.

'Drop you in the pool,' Morgan responded promptly.

'No! I'll get all wet.'

'That's the general idea.'

Stretching out her arm, Lyn caught hold of the rail at the side of the companionway just as he was about to climb it, and brought him to a stop. 'I have a better idea,' she said softly.

There was a lamp nearby, its mellow glow giving just enough light to illuminate the flight of stairs. Morgan turned his head quickly to look at her and caught his breath as he saw the desire in her eyes. 'Lyn.' He said her name on a thick, unsteady note.

Letting go of the rail, she put her arm round his neck, and with her other hand gently touched his face, her fingers soft against his skin. 'Why don't we go to the sun-lounge?' she breathed.

'You don't know what you're saying,' Morgan said

on a rough note.

'Oh, but I do.' And Lyn gently touched her mouth against his, her lips moist and sensuous.

She felt a quiver run through him, but he didn't close his eyes and kiss her, instead looking into her face and making no response. Lyn drew back, beginning to be afraid that he would reject her, but then he made a small, groaning sound deep in his throat and turned to carry her in the other direction, towards the sun-lounge at the stern.

It was empty, the other passengers all engrossed in their game of bridge. The light was on but Lyn reached out, as she had done before, and turned it off. For a few moments Morgan continued to hold her, but then he slowly set her on her feet, letting her body travel down the length of his as he did so, afterwards keeping his hands on her waist. He gazed down at her intently, and for a couple of seconds Lyn felt strangely nervous, and the smile she gave him trembled uncertainly on her lips.

Morgan gave an untidy sigh, as if he was annoyed with himself, but pulled her to him. 'Come here, brat,' he commanded.

His lips were hard, almost rough at first, and Lyn had the strange feeling that he was kissing her against his will, but soon she was lost to everything except the chaotic bewilderment of her own senses as he aroused emotions in her that she had only briefly glimpsed before with other men. Her head whirled, and there was no reality outside the hot demands of his mouth, the pressure of his body against hers, and the leaping fires that grew inside her and became all-consuming.

When he finally raised his head, Lyn found that she

was clinging to Morgan's shoulders, her senses giddy and her legs too weak to hold her. His own breathing was a little ragged, too, but after a moment Morgan grinned down at her bemused face. 'You look like a sixteen-year-old who's been kissed for the first time.'

'D-do I?' She tried to pull herself together, realising for a devastating instant of bitter regret that it hadn't been the same for Morgan as it had for her. For him it must only have been just another kiss: pleasant, but hardly a world-shattering experience.

His eyes grew sombre and he lifted a finger to trace the outline of her parted lips. 'But then, you are very young, aren't you?'

'But I'll get older,' Lyn pointed out. She moved closer to him, holding her thighs against his. 'And I'm old enough,' she added huskily.

The contact made Morgan draw in his breath sharply and put his hands low on either side of her waist. But he didn't push her away. 'One minute you act like a spoilt teenager, the next like a woman with a world of experience,' he said in an almost exasperated voice. 'So how am I supposed to treat you?'

'Like a woman,' she answered in fierce urgency. '*Please.*'

'Oh, Lyn.' Lifting his hand, Morgan put it behind her head, his fingers twining in her hair. His eyes holding hers, he pulled her slowly towards him, then lowered his head to kiss her again. Its effect was the same, only better, because this time he began to caress her, his free hand moving over her back, hard and hot against her bare skin. She gave a long sigh of utter delight, her mouth opening under his to let him explore and taste as he wanted. Such utter surrender could only arouse his own awareness, and Morgan kissed her with increasing passion, his hand stroking, his skilled fingers sending wave upon wave of delight coursing through her veins.

Lyn returned his kiss avidly, her senses on fire, all reason lost. She had never felt this way before and somehow knew deep inside her that she would never feel the same with anyone else. Morgan drew back and let her go, and she suddenly felt lost and empty, but he only lifted down one of the loungers. He sat on it and pulled her down on to his lap, his lips seeking her throat and leaving a trail of heat across her skin. Reaching up, he pushed aside the thin straps of her top and slid them down her arms, revealing the soft roundness of her breasts, her skin turned to silver in the moonlight, their curves emphasised by the shadows of the night. Lyn moaned when he touched her. Her body arched towards him and he bent to kiss her, his mouth lifting her to a frenzy of frustrated desire.

It was a while before he lifted his head, but when he did he took her mouth in a sudden burst of fierce passion that left her breathless, her body quivering. Her arms tight around his neck, Lyn clung to him for a long moment, then said, 'Morgan,' on a shuddering sigh.

'Yes?'

'Nothing. Just—just Morgan.'

He gave a small smile and pulled the straps of her top back on her shoulders, then stroked her hair back from her damp forehead.

'Why did you do that?' she asked on a puzzled, disappointed note.

He laughed. 'Do you always show your feelings like this?'

Looking into his eyes, Lyn said, with simple sincerity, 'I've never felt like this before.'

His hand stilled as their gaze held, but then Morgan lifted her off his lap and got quickly to his feet. 'You'd better go back to the passenger deck.'

'Aren't you coming?' she asked uncertainly.

'I'll be along.'

Turning his back on her, Morgan leaned on the rail and watched the white phosphorescence of the sea-spray gradually diminish into the far darkness of the night. Lyn looked at his broad back, wanting to run and put her arms round him, but feeling that he had deliberately shut her out. Slowly she turned and walked away.

Some of the passengers were out by the pool, having a nightcap. One of them offered her a drink but Lyn refused politely and went straight to her cabin. She shut the door and was about to lock it when she hesitated, wondering if Morgan might come to her later when everyone was in bed. After a long moment of inner turmoil she left it on the latch and got ready for bed. It seemed to take ages for the ship to settle down for the night. She heard people go past her cabin on the way to their own, and she thought she heard Morgan's voice saying goodnight and the sound of his door closing. Lying awake, with just a thin sheet over her, Lyn listened to the noises which had become so familiar that she hardly noticed them any more: the low groan of the engines, the waves slapping against the side . . . but the sound she strained to hear didn't come. Morgan's door stayed firmly shut and the tense excitement gradually faded until she drifted into sleep.

Usually when Lyn woke in the mornings she felt full of energy and jumped straight out of bed to dress and go and have breakfast on deck, but the next morning she lay in bed, thinking of the night before and trying to work things out in her mind. For her, it had been the most sensual experience she had ever known, but she put that thought aside for later; at the moment it was Morgan's reaction she wanted to define. She forced herself to admit, first of all, that he was far more experienced and therefore must find making love to her pretty mundane. And yet—her mind went back to the fierceness of some of his kisses, and she was sure there would be bruises on her skin where his fingers had tightened in sudden passion. He certainly wasn't immune to her, that was for sure, Lyn thought with a glow of satisfaction. But he hadn't followed it up by coming to her room last night. Her thoughts always came back to that, making her feel uncertain again, and eventually she got up and put on a bikini with shorts and a shirt over it.

Morgan was already out by the pool, wearing just a pair of shorts and sitting with one of the male passengers, chatting over a cup of coffee about cars, it sounded like. He looked up as Lyn walked over to them and gave her a keen glance. 'You've missed breakfast. Can I get you anything?'

'No, thanks.'

She went to turn away and go to an empty lounger on the other side of the pool, but Morgan reached out and caught her hand. 'Here, take mine.' He stood up and winked at her, then, to Lyn's startled pleasure, bent to kiss her on the mouth. She flushed and gave a quick, darting glance round to see that there were several interested onlookers. Bets, she thought, will be collected in after this.

Going to the other side of the pool, Morgan easily lifted a heavy fibreglass lounger and carried it over, his muscles rippling in the sun. He set it down beside hers so that she was between him and the other passenger and it was impossible to have any private talk. After a quarter of an hour or so she got bored by this and went in for a swim, but when she came out the man's wife had tactfully taken him away.

Heaving herself out, Lyn sat on the side of the pool, her legs dangling in the water, and reached up to wring the water out of her hair. Morgan ambled over and sat down beside her, his body hot against the coolness of hers.

'Why did you kiss me just now?' she demanded abruptly.

'Didn't you want me to?' He turned his head to look at her, his eyes narrowed against the sun.

'Yes, very much. But you've never done it before.'

'What happened last night hadn't happened before.'

She studied his face, trying to read his thoughts. There was so much she wanted to say, wanted to ask, but was too inexperienced to know how to go about it tactfully, and was afraid of annoying him, of making him change his mood. But as if he guessed, Morgan took hold of her hand nearest him and began to play with her wet fingers, then said, 'After you went to your cabin last night, I did a lot of thinking.'

'About—about us?' Lyn asked anxiously.

'What else?' Leaning forward he kissed the end of

her nose. 'You ought to put some cream on that or it will get burnt.'

'Yes, I will,' she promised impatiently. 'What did you think about us?'

He gave a crooked grin. 'Just that I thought I'd kiss you this morning.'

'In front of everyone?'

He nodded. 'Mm.'

'Which means?'

'Which means. . .' He shrugged. 'That we see how things go from here, I suppose.'

'But they *are* going somewhere?' Lyn asked on a note of happiness.

'I wouldn't have kissed you otherwise.'

'Oh, I see.' She looked at him teasingly. 'Kiss me again,' she ordered.

Morgan's left eyebrow rose. 'So it's sex on demand already, is it? I can see you're going to be a very demanding woman.' But he leaned forward to kiss her lingeringly on the mouth.

Lyn's thudding heart gradually subsided and she said unsteadily, 'I liked that.'

A shadow flickered in his eyes. 'You're so young, so trusting.'

'Shouldn't I trust you, then?'

He gave her a brooding look. 'That's something you will have to work out for yourself.' Lyn was about to ask him what he meant, when, in a mercurial change of mood, Morgan's eyes narrowed and he said, 'I seem to remember I was going to punish you last night.' And getting quickly to his feet he lifted her up and, before she could do more than give a scream, threw her into the pool!

From that moment their relationship really became a relationship. As the ship steamed its way past the tourist beaches of Tunisia towards Tunis, and then on to Algiers and Gibraltar, Morgan openly demonstrated that they were close, putting his arm round her and often kissing her before the others. And in the evenings when they were at sea they would sneak away to the sun-lounge where Morgan would kiss and caress her with a passion that seemed to grow with every kiss. But when they were in port they went on all the shore excursions with the other passengers and some of the crew, and nearly always ended up in a nightclub where the cabaret was invariably yet more belly-dancers.

When they reached Gibraltar the women put their collective foot down and refused to watch another belly-dancer. 'Not to worry,' Tim Browning reassured them soothingly. 'I know a place that doesn't have them.' And then caused a near mutiny when they ended up watching flamenco dancers instead.

But despite this they all had a great time that night. The voyage was far from over, but this was the last port of call before they reached England, which seemed to give an almost frenetic feel to the evening, as if it had to be made memorable. When they got back to the ship one couple caused a great deal of hilarity by attempting an impromptu flamenco dance themselves, but it could all have been ruined by a nasty little incident when the third mate, who was more than a little tight, tried to dance with Lyn, holding her much too tightly, and refusing to let go when she protested. But Morgan dealt with it most efficiently by simply picking the man up by his collar and trouser-belt and dropping him in the shallow end of the pool.

'Morgan's so macho,' one of the women said admiringly to Lyn, as she watched the sailor being fished out by his laughing friends. She turned to give Lyn a speculative look and asked a question she was longing to ask but would probably never have dared to if she'd been completely sober. 'I bet he's absolutely fantastic in bed, isn't he?'

Her cheeks flaming red in the darkness, Lyn muttered an incoherent reply and walked away. It was a question she would never have answered anyway, even if she'd known the answer. But she didn't, because, even though their evenings in the privacy of the sun-lounge had been pretty passionate, Morgan had never followed them up, had never carried their lovemaking to the logical, and in Lyn's case increasingly longed-for, conclusion. Morgan knew how she felt, of course—it was impossible for him not to when he held her quivering body in his arms and she moaned in mingled frustration and excitement, unable to stand what he was doing to her and yet longing to be closer still.

Her feelings about it were a crazy mixture. Sometimes she was glad that he was taking it slowly, so that each new discovery of each other became the sweeter; at others, when her emotions reached fever pitch, she longed for him to take her now, *now*. And sometimes, when she lay lonely and frustrated in her bed, feelings of inadequacy overwhelmed her and she wondered if it was her inexperience that put him off. Perhaps Morgan was afraid of becoming too involved with her, that if he went the whole way he would commit himself to a relationship that he didn't particularly want and she was too immature to handle. If so, she ought to be grateful to him, she supposed. He obviously wasn't in love with her and didn't want to hurt her. Perhaps to him it was just a holiday romance, a pleasant diversion to while away the long voyage, but something he was going to make darn sure didn't tie him down when they got back to England.

Although reason told her she ought to be grateful, her emotions and overwhelming need for him soon drowned out common sense. When did love and common sense ever go hand in hand? For Lyn was sure that she was in love with Morgan. What else could this overwhelming longing be, this tightness in her chest whenever she saw him, and this total inability to think of a future without him? More than once she'd sternly told herself that it was just sex, that she would grow out of it—but her heart told her that wasn't true. She wanted to be with Morgan, always, and in every sense of the word.

During their stay in Gibraltar, as in every other port of call, Morgan had gone alone to the main post office in the town, and Lyn was fairly certain that he had been in touch with her father. But if he had he never mentioned it to her, and she never asked, feeling that somehow it would spoil things if she did. That world had receded far into the background and she pushed all thought of it to the back of her mind—another symptom of the *mañana* seductiveness of the voyage.

From Gibraltar the ship made its way up the coast of Portugal and Spain, the sun still shining from a sky that seemed eternally blue that summer. But as it rounded the northern coast of Spain and turned into the Bay of Biscay, the sky became cloudy and grey, and the wind grew fresh, blowing from the west.

'Are you a good sailor?' Morgan asked Lyn as he looked out at the lowering horizon.

Lyn shivered, feeling cold after the heat of the sun. 'I have been up to now.'

'That was nothing,' Morgan said dismissively. 'The Med is a millpond compared to an ocean. But it looks as if there's a storm blowing up now.'

'I don't know, then,' Lyn said, and she turned a bright, expectant face up to his. 'But it will be interesting to find out.'

Putting his arms round her to hug her, Morgan laughed and said, 'That's my girl.'

'Am I?' She looked into his eyes earnestly. 'Am I your girl?'

'Of course. What else?' But he spoke lightly and she was unable to believe him.

The wind increased as the day wore on and only two of the other passengers beside themselves appeared at dinner that evening. The master stayed on the bridge, but Tim joined them and cheerfully told them they were in for a bit of a blow.

Somewhat to her surprise, Lyn found that she was enjoying the storm. After dinner she and Morgan borrowed some waterproofs and went out on the deck. At first it was difficult to keep her balance on the heaving surface and she had to hold on to a rail or on to Morgan, whichever was most handy, but gradually she got her sea legs and was able to brace herself against the motion of the ship. It wasn't late, only about nine o'clock, but the sunset was lost behind the clouds, the night already a dark turmoil. And it was so loud out here, the noise beating at her eardrums, the heavy seas thudding against the ship's sides as if they were hitting a solid object, and sometimes it felt as if they'd gone straight into a concrete wall as the ship was brought up shudderingly against a huge swell. The wind tore at them, whipping Lyn's hair out from under the sou'wester, howling round the deck cargo, and sending spray that wet them even more than the pouring rain.

'Are you all right? Do you want to go back inside?' Morgan shouted at her.

'No! I think it's great.' She turned an excited but wet face up to him.

'Come up in the bow, then.'

Holding her in a steely grip, Morgan took her to the front of the ship and put his arms round her, holding firmly on to the rail in a spot that was partly sheltered from the wind. There they watched in fascination as the sky completely blackened and thunder clapped around them. Lyn gasped as lightning darted across the sky, but it was a gasp of awed excitement, not fear. She loved the storm and was fascinated by its primeval power, the fragility of their little ship in its path completely forgotten.

Despite their waterproofs they were soon wet but neither of them felt cold and they went on standing there until a lightning bolt came very close and Lyn involuntarily shrank back closer to Morgan, then turned and laughed aloud. His arms tightened and then he was kissing her fiercely, the taste of the sea on his lips, the tang of it strong in her nostrils. He kissed her

avidly, the power of the storm rousing some equally
basic instinct in him. He muttered words against her
mouth, which she couldn't hear above the wind, but it
didn't matter—the devouring need in his kiss was
words enough.

Suddenly he scooped her up in his arms and using
his powerful muscles carried her along the rolling
deck and through a door into the interior of the ship.
The heavy door clanged shut behind them and it
immediately felt as if she'd gone deaf, the noise was
so much less. But Morgan gave her little time to notice
because he was kissing her again as he strode
purposefully down the corridor and up to the
passenger deck. The place was deserted, all the
passengers in their cabins, weathering out the storm
as well as their stomachs would allow. Morgan pushed
open the door of Lyn's cabin and carried her inside,
still taking her mouth in greedy, compulsive kisses.

There was a heightened excitement in him—Lyn
could feel it as he set her down and pulled her close to
him, his shoulders hunching as he held her close. Then
his hands were on her waterproofs, throwing them
aside, pulling off the sou'wester, his own joining them
in a dripping heap on the floor. Putting his hands on
either side of her head, he rained kisses on her wet
face, then came back to her lips with such intensity
that she whimpered in joy and anticipation. His hands
went to her clothes, tearing them in his haste, and then
he was loving her with his hands, his mouth. In an
agony of delight, Lyn reached down to hold his wet
head, her fingers rigid. She cried out as he knelt before
her, her head arching back, her sensuous cry lost

beneath the thunder of the storm. And then she was pulling at his shirt, as aroused as he, her hands shaking in quivering excitement.

His skin was initially cold to her touch but soon grew heated as her fingers ran over him, exploring in delight his firm muscles, the strength of his chest. He held her naked body against his, his legs braced to keep them upright as the ship pitched and rolled. Lyn moved against him sensuously, the fires deep inside taking control, teaching her the primeval lessons of love. Morgan groaned, the sound coming from deep inside his chest, his fingers digging into the soft flesh of her hips. Lifting his hand, he put it behind her head and ground out her name on a long, questioning note of hungry yearning.

Her eyes were heavy-lidded with desire, but she opened them enough to see his blue eyes blazing at her, to recognise the fiery need in his gaze. 'Yes,' she breathed. 'Oh, Morgan, yes, yes.'

He gave a cry of triumph and lifted her against him, held her there to let her feel the power and strength of his manhood, then carried her in one swift stride to the bed.

About them the storm continued to rage but it was as nothing to the storm of sexual pleasure and excitement that filled the little cabin that night. Morgan's lovemaking lifted Lyn to peak after peak of ecstasy like the waves breaking against a shore, and his own cries of conquering pleasure mingled with the crash of the thunderclaps. They made love long into the night, and, as they lay in each other's arms, satiated at last, so the storm lessened and died and peace came with the dawn of a new day.

CHAPTER FOUR

TILTING her head towards the early morning sky, Lyn felt the soft rain on her face. It had a quality all its own, that rain, a fresh, sweet smell and feel to it that told her she was home again at last. The end of the voyage was growing closer now, as close as the long grey coastline with the rich green fields beyond. She stood on the main deck, her arms on the rail, almost glad to be alone for a while. The past week had been so wonderful, sometimes Lyn couldn't believe that it was possible to be so happy. She was head over heels in love with Morgan, that was certain, and her doubts about the way he felt about her had receded far to the back of her mind. Surely no man could make love to her as hungrily and as sensuously as he did and not be emotionally involved?

She put out her tongue to catch some raindrops and smiled as she tasted them. English rain: it even had a taste all its own. There were no qualms in her mind now about seeing her father again. She felt ready to face him, to face whatever life held for her. All thanks to Morgan, of course. Loving him, and being made love to by him, had given her such confidence in herself again that she felt like a new person. Like a woman, she supposed. An adult instead of a girl. Her mirror even told her that she looked different; she had looked fit and healthy before, but now there was an inner radiance, a light of happiness deep in her eyes

74

that told the world she was in love.

Only one thing detracted from complete happiness: she still resisted Morgan's efforts to persuade her to accept Claire, her father's second wife. The hatred that had festered for over a year went too deep and, even though she thought she would do anything for Morgan, she couldn't bring herself to agree to that. And she even rather resented his asking her to; she didn't want him to even think about the woman who had caused her and her mother so much unhappiness. Whenever he mentioned Claire she got uptight, even angry, feeling a great surge of an emotion that was very close to jealousy. 'Don't let's talk about her,' she said, her lower lip thrusting forward petulantly. Putting her arms round his neck, Lyn would kiss him with the certainty of intimacy and power, and Morgan would reluctantly let himself be seduced into a change of mood.

A tug came out into the estuary to meet them and guide them into Tilbury Docks, the land very close now. Lyn hadn't bothered to make any plans for when they left the ship; wherever Morgan went she would go: life was as simple as that now. There was the sound of a metal door closing behind her and she turned to smile at him as Morgan came to join her. 'All fixed?' she asked.

'Yes, the captain has agreed to unload the Rolls first. We'll have to clear it through Customs, of course, but the papers are all in order so that shouldn't take too long.' He put his arm round her. 'Aren't you cold standing out here in the rain?'

'No.' But she snuggled up to him all the same.

Morgan grinned at her and kissed her in a casual way that she liked because it showed that they were close, so close that he could kiss her any time he chose and in public. It spelt out that they were lovers, and Lyn was so proud of him that she wanted the whole world to know. Everyone on the ship certainly did; Morgan had tried to be discreet, but the way Lyn had looked at him after that first night together, and even more the way she had needed to be close to him and touch him, had immediately given their secret away. 'You look as if you're on your honeymoon,' one of the women passengers had told her. And Lyn had smiled, realising that was exactly how she felt.

'It shouldn't take us more than an hour to drive into central London once we're through Customs,' Morgan remarked now.

Turning her back to the rail, Lyn looked along the length of the ship. 'I shall be sorry to leave this old tub. The good ship *British Bounty*. This voyage has been—quite an experience.' And she smiled into his eyes.

'Hasn't it just?' And Morgan bent to kiss her on the nose.

'Where will we go—to your place?'

He grimaced. 'My place is just a small service flat, hardly suitable for you.'

'Does it have a bed?' she asked, her voice softening in unknowing wantonness.

Morgan grinned, recognising the change in her. 'Yes, it does. But it's only a single bed and I'm growing tired of trying to make love to you in single beds; it cramps my style.'

'I hadn't noticed,' she answered pertly.

'But you will when I get you in a king-size. Especially one that doesn't roll around all the time.'

And he kissed her on the nose again.

'I can't wait,' she said, meaning it.

Looking into her face, Morgan said, 'You're quite something, you know that?'

Lyn raised an eyebrow. 'I'm grateful for the compliment, but what exactly does it mean?'

'That taking you to bed was—quite a revelation.'

'I turned out to be rather a hot number, huh?'

Morgan gave a laugh of deep enjoyment. 'And some.'

'So where are we going to find this king-size bed?'

'I'll book you into a hotel.'

'You mean you'll book *us* into a hotel.'

But he shook his head, sending a sudden sharp *frisson* of fear running through her at even the thought of being apart from him. 'No, I have to deliver the Rolls to my friend.'

'But surely you can do that tomorrow?'

'I don't want to chance any damage being done to it in London, not after I've got it all this way in one piece.'

'Where does your friend live? I'll come with you,' Lyn said eagerly.

But Morgan again shook his head. 'I don't think that's a good idea. I'll stay overnight with my friend and phone you when I get back to London tomorrow morning. Besides,' he gave a twisted kind of smile, 'you'll want to contact your father today, and it would hardly do for me to be staying with you in a hotel, would it?'

'I don't care if he knows,' Lyn said immediately.

Morgan straightened up. 'You may feel differently when you've been home a little while.' She opened her mouth to make a swift denial but he put a long finger over her lips. 'But, in any case, I want you to promise me, Lyn, that you won't let your father find out that we're—close. Do you understand?'

'No.'

'He might come after me with a shotgun!' he said with a shudder of mock terror.

She looked at him tensely. 'Don't laugh at me. I—I want to be with you, Morgan.'

Reaching out he put his hand on her shoulder. 'Talk to your father. Sort things out with him before you make any other plans.' He hesitated, seemed about to say something else, then changed his mind. 'We have plenty of time,' he said instead. 'Give yourself some space, Lyn. You don't have to rush into any decisions.'

She stared at him, a tiny fear in her heart again, but then remembered about the king-size bed. He wouldn't have said that unless he meant to be with her again soon.

Their privacy was invaded by some of the other passengers who joined them then to watch the ship being brought into its mooring. After that there were farewells to be said, promises to keep in touch made that would soon be forgotten, and a round of goodbyes to the master and the crew.

Lyn went ashore with her luggage and watched as the Rolls was carefully lowered on to firm ground again. Not that it felt very firm; that was the trouble with being on the sea for any length of time: once you went ashore you lost your sense of balance and it felt as if the ground were moving under you. When Morgan joined her, Lyn turned a white face up to him. 'I feel landsick,' she complained.

He laughed and put her luggage into the boot of the

Rolls. It didn't take long to clear Customs and soon they were threading their way through streets busy with rush-hour traffic, Morgan driving carefully along.

'The steering wheel is on the wrong side for England,' Lyn remarked. 'Will your friend have it changed round?'

Morgan gave her a laughing glance. 'If he did that it wouldn't be a collector's item any more. The car's curiosity value lies in the fact that it's one of a very limited number of this model, the Silver Dawn, that was made only for the North American export market.'

'How did it get to Israel, then?'

'Presumably someone bought it in America and had it shipped out there.'

'And now you've brought it back full circle to England where it was made. You've brought it home.' Lyn smiled, liking the idea. 'Just as you've brought me home.'

'Mm.' Morgan reached across and squeezed her hand, but Lyn noticed that, for the first time since they had become lovers, there was again a small frown between Morgan's eyes.

He took her to a hotel near Hyde Park, but left once he'd made her promise to phone her father straight away. 'He'll be waiting for your call.'

Lyn promised, but she took a leisurely bath and washed her hair before she sat down on the big double bed, a bath-sheet wrapped round her, and picked up the phone with reluctant hands. She rang her father at his office and was connected to him within seconds. It felt so strange to hear his voice again. Silly tears came into Lyn's eyes, and her father sounded as emotional as she was. The tone of his letter had told her that he missed her, but even so she wasn't prepared for the warmth in his voice, especially as they had parted on such bad terms. She promised to meet him for lunch at their favourite Italian restaurant that he had been taking her to ever since she was a child, and rushed to get ready. Her clothes, however, made her grimace; she had bought very few while she was away and what she had were hardly suitable for a wet day in England. Fashions, too, had changed—Lyn had noticed that as they were driving along, and, as she desperately wanted to look her best for Morgan, it became imperative that she went out and bought some new clothes as soon as possible. In the meantime, clean jeans and a sweater would have to do.

By the time she was ready the clouds had lifted and a watery sun was trying to break through, so she decided to walk instead of taking a cab. The West End streets were full of tourists and office workers beginning their lunch break. Lyn looked at the girls, comparing their bright, smart beauty to those she had seen in the countries she'd visited. I'm definitely going to have to smarten myself up if I'm going to compete, she realised. She so wanted Morgan to be proud of her. She wanted to be sophisticated and elegant for him, to be everything that he could ever want in a woman. The shop windows full of beautiful clothes almost tempted Lyn inside half a dozen times, but she managed to resist, eager now to meet her father and not wanting to be late.

He was waiting for her in the small upstairs bar of the restaurant and sprang to his feet when she hurried in. For a few seconds she was shy and didn't know what to do, but then he opened his arms and she ran into them, hugging him tightly. He returned the embrace with equal fervour, kissed her and then stood back to look at her.

'You're so tanned!' he exclaimed. 'You look wonderful. Kibbutz life must have done you good.'

Lyn thanked him but was inwardly amazed at the change in him. He looked so different. During the marriage to her mother he had gradually put on weight until he looked quite tubby, and his hair had definitely begun to grow grey even though he wasn't yet fifty, but now he had slimmed right down and there was only a faint hint of grey at the sides of his well-cut hair. He looked a good ten years younger than he had before she went away. She remarked on it and he laughed and said, 'Oh, that's Claire's doing. She encourages me to——' He broke off as he saw the stony look that came into Lyn's face. For a moment there was an awkward silence between them, but then Mario, the head waiter, came up and greeted them like old friends, and the little hiatus was glossed over.

But it wasn't the only awkward moment during the meal; almost every line of conversation seemed to lead to a sensitive subject. When they talked about old friends it became clear that he had visited them with Claire, and she felt resentful that her mother had been supplanted. And he seemed to have lots of new interests, too, making her realise that his life had completely changed.

'Where is Mother?' she asked him.

'In Australia, last I heard. Visiting her new husband's

relations and touring the country on an extended honeymoon.' He took his wallet from his pocket and took out a sheet of paper. 'This is a telephone number where you can leave a message for your mother, or else they'll tell you how to get in touch with her.'

Slowly Lyn reached out and took it. 'Whose number is it?'

'Her husband's eldest son's, I think.' He gave a glance at her shocked face. 'Oh, yes, he has children. So I suppose that makes him your stepfather and the children your stepbrothers and sisters, doesn't it?' He laughed shortly. 'From having a small family, you now seem to be part of a greatly extended one, Lyn.'

'They're not my family,' she answered sharply. 'You and Mother are the only family I have or will ever want.'

Her father gave a small sigh. 'I see you haven't changed.' Quickly he changed the subject yet again. 'How was the voyage?'

'Great. The weather was perfect, and I enjoyed the slow journey from country to country, although I didn't think I would at the start.'

'And how did you get on with Morgan French?' he asked, his eyes suddenly intent.

'Morgan?' Her face lit as she said his name, the radiance completely giving the lie to her studiedly casual, 'Oh, OK, I guess.'

Jonathan Standish's eyes widened as he looked at his daughter, then a thoughtful gleam came into them, but he merely said, 'And what do you intend to do with yourself now you're home? You are, of course, very welcome to come back to live with me and Claire, but somehow I think that idea will still be just as unpopular.'

'Yes, it is,' Lyn agreed definitely. 'What happened to the flat Mother took?'

'She resold the lease when she got engaged to her Australian. All the things you left there she sent over to me to look after for you.'

'Then I'll have to look for a place of my own.'

'Well, your twenty-first birthday is coming up; if you like, I'll buy you a flat as your present, and of course you'll still have your monthly allowance.'

'Maybe I ought to get a job,' she offered.

Her father laughed in surprised amusement, which suddenly angered her. 'That's hardly necessary.'

'Why not?' she retorted bitterly. 'With that gold-digger of a wife that you've got, you'll want all your money to meet her demands for jewels and clothes. And I bet she'll have something to say when she finds out you're offering me a flat for my——'

'Lyn, stop it!' Jonathan Standish broke in harshly. 'Why do you still hate her so? Surely by now you'll have come to terms with——'

'You *know* why.'

'Didn't Morgan speak to you about Claire?'

She gave him a surprised look, remembering just how often Morgan had brought up the unwelcome subject. Her surprise changed to uncertainty as she said, 'Why, yes, he did. Did *you* tell him to?'

'I asked him to try to reconcile you to my marriage if he got the opportunity, yes,' her father admitted. He sighed. 'But it doesn't seem to have done any good.'

'No. Nothing will,' Lyn stated with finality.

He gave her a brooding look, then shrugged. 'So be it. I'm not going to let it come between us.'

Her face broke into a happy smile. 'Good, I'm glad. We can still see each other without *her*, can't we?' Lyn just stopped herself from saying 'that woman'.

'If you insist.'

'And if she allows you to,' Lyn said shrewdly.

He gave a short laugh. 'It isn't easy for a man to be caught between two loves, Lyn. My love for you and my love for Claire.'

'But not love for Mother,' she said flatly.

'I shall always be extremely fond of your mother, Lyn, but we had fallen out of love with each other long before Claire came along.'

'I don't believe that; it's just what you want to believe, a sop for your conscience. *She* split you up and ruined Mummy's life.'

'Well, it hardly seems to be ruined now, does it?' he answered shortly, and lifted his hand to attract the waiter's attention for the bill.

When they got outside on the pavement he hailed a taxi, saying, 'Phone me any time you need me; and let me know when you find a flat. Can I drop you off at your hotel?'

Lyn shook her head. 'Thanks, but I need to get my hair done and I have lots of clothes to buy,' she told him, excitement in her voice as she thought of who she was buying them to please.

Looking at her, her father commented, 'You look as if you're in love.'

'Do I?' Her face softened, her eyes glowing as she gave a delighted laugh. 'What on earth gives you that idea? I'm just glad to be home and that we've patched things up, that's all.'

She waved him goodbye and spent the rest of the afternoon very happily, first in a hairdressing salon and afterwards in an orgy of shopping, and the evening in trying everything on again before the mirror and wondering if Morgan would like it. Ever since she had got back to the hotel Lyn had been expecting Morgan to ring, but it became evening and he still hadn't, so she decided to eat in the hotel, telling the reception desk where to find her. It was stupid of her not to have asked Morgan where his friend lived; it could be up in Yorkshire or somewhere for all she knew, but he must surely have reached it by now. Unless he was having trouble with the car. When ten o'clock came round and he still hadn't phoned, Lyn convinced herself that he must have had a terrible accident and be lying in a hospital bed somewhere. And she had no idea which direction he'd taken so she could phone the police and find out.

Too anxious to sleep very much that night, Lyn started going through all the M. Frenches in the London Telephone Directory first thing in the morning, catching people before they left for work. At some of the numbers she got no reply, so kept trying them during the course of the day, finally giving an almighty gasp of relief when one of the numbers was finally answered at about three in the afternoon and she heard Morgan's voice.

'Why didn't you call me?' she demanded. 'I've been frantic with worry about you. I was sure you'd had an accident.'

Surprised, Morgan said, 'I've only just got here. I

had to travel back to London by train.'

'But you could have called me yesterday.'

'What for?'

His answer brought her up short; just being away from him for half a day had made her miss him unbearably and she had longed just to hear his voice because she loved him so much. But that casual 'What for?' told a very different tale. He hadn't missed her at all, probably hadn't even given her a thought after he'd left her, and certainly hadn't felt any overwhelming need to call and reassure himself that she was OK and to hear her voice again.

'Lyn, are you still there?' Morgan asked after a long moment.

'Yes, I'm still here,' she answered stiltedly. 'I thought you would have been interested in how I got on with my father.'

'So how did you?'

'OK, I suppose.'

'Is that all? Just "OK"?'

'He offered to buy me a flat for my birthday. He also told me that he'd ordered you to try to bring me round to accepting Claire,' she added shortly.

'Which was a complete waste of effort,' Morgan said wryly, making no attempt to deny it.

'Why didn't you tell me?'

'What would have been the point?' he said dismissively, and very effectively changed the subject by adding, 'How big is the bed in your room?'

She smiled. 'Definitely king-size.'

'Good. How about dinner tonight? I'll call for you at eight.'

'Not till then?' Lyn said wistfully.

'Sorry, sweetheart, but I have things to do this afternoon after being away so long.'

'Yes, of course.' She managed to laugh. 'I guess I've just got so used to being with you all day long. OK, see you at eight. I'll wait for you in the bar.'

She dressed to stun in a cream silk number that left one shoulder of her golden-tanned body bare. And she knew that she had succeeded when, deliberately late, she walked into the room and Morgan slowly straightened up from where he was leaning against the bar, his eyes fixed on her as she paused in the doorway.

Lyn stood there for a moment longer and let her eyes flick over the room, noting the sudden drop in the noise level as men noticed her, then she walked straight across to Morgan, put a hand on his shoulder, and kissed him lingeringly on the mouth. He returned the kiss, a familiar hand at her waist, then looked down at her, devils of mischievous amusement in his blue eyes. 'What are you trying to do?' he murmured in her ear. 'Compromise me?'

Tilting her head she looked back at him with a seductive pout on her lips. 'Yes.'

He laughed aloud. 'You look fantastic. A world away from the nubile young girl I used to chase round the deck.'

He bought her a drink and they left shortly afterwards to go to the restaurant where Morgan had booked a table. 'Was your friend pleased with the car?' Lyn asked him when they were seated.

'Very. He's going to show it at a Rolls-Royce rally next month along with a couple of his other cars, and has asked me to go along and drive it.'

Lyn waited for him to invite her to go with him, but when he didn't she said, over-brightly, 'That sounds like fun.'

'Mm. When are you going to start looking for a flat?'

She gave a small shrug. 'Next week, I suppose.' She stole a look at him from under her lashes, aware of an inner abstraction about him, as if his mind was on something else. 'Will you help me look—or do you have to work?'

'I've a mountain of correspondence that was waiting for me at my flat to be dealt with,' he answered obliquely.

'But you don't have to work?' She gave him a direct look. 'You never have told me what you do for a living. Please tell me now.'

His left eyebrow rising at her firm tone, Morgan said, 'Is it that important?'

'I think so. You can learn a lot about a man from his work.'

'You already know a lot about me,' he reminded her, a provocative look in his blue eyes.

Lyn flushed but said determinedly, 'Don't change the subject. I want to know what you do.'

Morgan's mouth twisted a little and he sat back in his chair. 'All right. I suppose you might call me a drop-out.'

Lyn's mouth fell open. 'But you *can't* be.'

'Why not?'

'Because you can't, that's all. You're not the type. You're too intelligent. And you must surely have ambitions?'

'I used to have,' Morgan admitted. 'I used to be a stockbroker with all the trappings: a Porsche, an apartment in a converted warehouse by the river, and the luxury lifestyle to go with them. I was the archetypal yuppie,' he said on a hollow note. 'Then the crash came and the bottom dropped out of the share market.'

'You mean you were fired?' Lyn asked in horror.

Morgan gave a short laugh and shook his head. 'No, I was the one who did all the firing. And it wasn't pleasant. Men older than myself with families, young men knocked off the first rungs of the ladder and having to start again, secretaries, tea-ladies. No, it definitely wasn't pleasant. It made me stop and take a good hard look at my life—and I didn't much like what I saw. I was often working a fifteen-hour day and weekends as well, most of it spent on the phone and in front of a computer. The job had taken me over and I was living to work instead of the other way round. So I decided to quit and take a sabbatical, give myself time to decide what I wanted to do with the rest of my life.'

'And have you decided?'

His eyes settled on her face for a moment and then flicked away. 'No.'

'Could you go back into business—if you wanted to?'

'I've had offers,' he admitted. His lips twisted. 'Is that what you think I ought to do?'

Lyn frowned and said carefully, 'I've always imagined that success in his chosen career is what any man would want. OK, so maybe it all got you down and you needed a break, but surely you don't want to—to just drift? You must want to get back into business.'

'How like your father you sound,' Morgan remarked with heavy irony.

'My father? Did he say the same sort of thing to you?'

'Almost identical. Would you like some more wine?'

'Yes, please.' Lyn looked at him unhappily, sensing his withdrawal and knowing that she'd said the wrong thing. 'What else could you do?' she asked to try to retrieve the situation.

He shrugged. 'Something a long way from London. Run a farm, perhaps.'

Her eyes widened. 'Do you know how to farm?'

'No, but I could learn.'

Lyn didn't say anything, but her face told him what she thought of the idea. Her family had been successful in business for the last three generations, building up quite an empire, and she had been brought up believing that a man didn't count for much unless he was a success. She could understand why Morgan had needed to get out for a while, but there was no way she could envisage his not going back. He was so confident, so capable. She guessed that he must have been brilliant at his job to have got to such a high position so young. No wonder people were trying to get him to go back.

'You obviously don't see me as a farmer,' he said with a wry laugh.

She shook her head. 'No, to be honest, I can't.'

Putting his knife and fork down on his still half-full plate, Morgan said, 'I thought that you would have understood, after running away to a kibbutz.' He refilled his wine glass and sat back, taking a deep drink.

'It was just somewhere to go, really. A girl I used to go to school with had been to one and she said it was fun. To be honest, I didn't expect to be there so long; I thought my parents would have found me long before my father sent you to bring me home.'

'Didn't you enjoy it there?'

'Yes, but—but it wasn't *me*, if you see what I mean.'

'Very clearly,' Morgan said sardonically, and took another drink.

The evening was going hopelessly wrong; Lyn knew it but couldn't do anything about it. Morgan seemed to be in such a strange mood and nothing she did could change it. She tried to amuse him and when that failed flirted with him, but the brooding lines around his mouth only deepened and he beckoned the waiter to bring over a second bottle of wine.

It wasn't until they were back at her hotel room that everything came right again. He caught hold of her the moment they entered the room, kissing her in hungry passion, then took her the first time with an almost savage abandon, not even giving her time to take her clothes off before he dragged Lyn down on to the bed, his lovemaking wild and uncontrolled. But afterwards, when she lay exhausted on the coverlet, Morgan reached out and drew her to him, holding her close and kissing her face, murmuring an apology. Reaching up, Lyn stroked his cheek, her hand shaking, her eyes dark pools of satiated ecstasy. He undressed her then and carried her into the bathroom, lying beside her in the double bath, kissing her, loving her. And later, as they lay in the big bed, he made love to her as he never had before, deliberately holding back his own excitement to lift her again and again to the dizzy heights of climactic rapture.

She cried out, her body arching, then subsided into his arms, tears of overwhelming emotion on her cheeks. 'I love you,' she breathed intensely. 'Oh, Morgan, I love you so much.'

Lifting himself on to his elbow, he looked down at her face. He seemed about to say something but Lyn clung to him fiercely. 'Don't ever leave me,' she begged him. 'Promise you won't ever leave me!'

Slowly, Morgan lifted a hand to brush away the hair that clung to her hot, damp forehead, and kissed her eyelids closed. 'I won't leave you,' he promised, and held her, staring into space, until she fell asleep in his arms.

During the next week Lyn rented a fully furnished flat until she could find a place of her own. Not that she had made much effort to find one. Morgan spent so much time with her that he had virtually moved in, although he still had his own place and went there from time to time. She was so happy: being with Morgan, going places with him, wearing all her new clothes. Lyn felt as if she was on a continuous high and failed to note the slightly grim quality beneath Morgan's apparent cheerfulness.

One day they had lunch with her father, at a restaurant in the City this time. It was her father's idea; Morgan hadn't been very keen, but Lyn could think of nothing nicer than to be with both of the men in her life. So she had her way and the meal went off very well until she noticed the little undercurrent of tension between the two men. It wasn't anything you could really put your finger on, just an unexpected emphasis on a word, the way Morgan's mouth twisted when her father talked of his company, and the glance they exchanged after Lyn leaned against Morgan's shoulder and smiled lovingly into his eyes, her feelings and their intimacy plain for all to see.

They spent every night together and most of their days, but that evening Morgan said he had to meet someone on business. 'But you'll come back tonight, won't you?' Lyn said, putting her arms round his neck.

'Hmm, I might.' And then, as she pushed her hips against his. 'Sex cat. As if I could keep away.'

But the evening passed and, when it got to the early hours of the morning, Lyn began to be afraid that he wouldn't come. It was never far below the surface, that fear, because she knew in her heart that she loved Morgan far more than he did her. If he loved her at all. If it wasn't just sex. He had never actually said that he loved her, even though he called her his darling, his sweetheart. But she knew that he cared and she clung on to that. And she tried hard to please him, to be the kind of woman that she thought he wanted; not only in bed but in their life together, too.

It was nearly three in the morning before she heard his key turn in the lock. Rushing out into the hall, she ran to him. 'Are you all right? I was so worried. What happened?'

'Nothing. I felt like a walk, that's all.'

'A walk?' She stared at him, knowing that something was wrong. 'Your—business meeting—didn't it come off?'

He glanced at her and gave a harsh laugh. 'Oh, yes, it came off OK. They made me an offer I couldn't refuse.'

There was such bitterness in his voice as he said it that Lyn gazed at him in consternation, hating to see him like this. 'Why? What do you mean?'

'What? Oh, nothing.' Shaking her off he went into the sitting-room and fixed himself a drink, taking it down in one deep swallow as if he needed it badly. He sat down in the armchair, and then held his hand out to her as he saw her worried frown. 'Come on, don't worry about it. It's nothing.'

She went quickly to sit on his lap, the silk of her pyjamas against the roughness of his suit. Almost absent-mindedly he began to caress her but then his hand stilled. 'Won't you tell me what happened?' Lyn pleaded. She hesitated, but when he didn't speak, said, 'You seem so strange tonight. You frighten me.'

At that his eyes flicked up to meet hers. 'Frighten you?'

'Yes. I—I want to share with you, your life, not only your—your bed,' she told him groping for the right words. 'But you're shutting me out. And I don't know why.' She tried to say the words calmly but behind them lay a great fear. She remembered a friend's bitter words after a broken affair, 'Men are quite capable of making sex look like love. Of having an extremely passionate affair and then just walking away from it—quite *dispassionately*. Men are fickle, they soon grow tired of what's offered to them on a plate.' And Lyn was terrified now that Morgan wanted to leave her. She looked down at him, her eyes wide and tense, pleading for reassurance.

He gave her an assessing look and for a moment she began to hope that he would confide in her, but then he turned his head away and reached out to pick up his drink. 'There's nothing to tell,' he said shortly. 'I was given a choice that was really no choice, that's all.'

'You won't—you won't have to go away, will you?'

'No, I won't have to go away.' But he said it heavily and it gave her no comfort.

Finishing his drink, Morgan looked at his watch. 'It's dreadfully late; I must let you get some sleep.' Putting his hands on her waist, he lifted her off his lap.

'Where are you going?'

'Back to my flat. I'll call you.' Perfunctorily, he kissed her on the nose and walked into the hall. He had almost reached the door when he heard Lyn call his name. 'Yes?' She didn't answer so he walked back to the sitting-room.

She was standing in the centre of the room, the cream silk of the pyjamas in a small glistening heap around her feet, her naked body like the bronze of an ancient goddess in the soft light of the lamp, her long fair hair caressing the soft swell of her breasts. 'Don't go,' she said softly.

Morgan caught his breath and stood for a moment gazing at her loveliness, then took two hasty strides across the room and caught her to him. 'You witch. I'm crazy about you.'

He went to pick her up and carry her into the bedroom, but Lyn stopped him and began to take off his clothes, doing it slowly so that by the time she'd finished he was fully aroused. She kissed him then, her lips exploring his skin, making him moan aloud, his fingers digging into her shoulders. 'Lyn, for God's sake. . .'

Straightening up, she put her hands on either side of his head and gazed tensely into his face. 'You promised you'd never leave me. You won't, will you?'

His lips twisted sardonically as Morgan looked back at her and Lyn knew that he had seen through this seduction scene, but, after a long, traumatic moment, he said on a terse, harsh note, 'We'd better get married, then, hadn't we?'

Lyn stared at him, her face filling with radiant joy. 'Do you mean it?' And then, quickly, in case he changed his mind, 'Oh, yes, we *certainly* had. Oh, Morgan!' She clung to him and wanted to tell him how happy she was and how much she loved him, but he took her mouth in fierce kisses and bore her down to the floor so that her senses soon drowned beneath the onslaught of his impassioned lovemaking.

Later, when they were in bed, Morgan fell into a deep, exhausted sleep, but Lyn lay awake, looking down at him in the light of the bedside lamp. At first she felt wildly, ecstatically happy; she was going to marry Morgan and the future stretched in front of her in a long, rosy glow. But as the night passed she remembered her parents' marriage and how it had so easily been broken. She also made herself admit what she already feared in her heart: that Morgan didn't love her as much as she loved him. I can make him love me as much, she thought fiercely. I know I can! But the dread of his one day leaving her, as her father had left her mother, filled her with terror.

Daylight was filtering through the curtains when Morgan finally awoke. Lyn was still sitting up in the bed, watching him, and she saw him blink, then recognise his surroundings. He saw her and began a lazy smile, but then he remembered and she saw his eyes shadow. A sharp stab of pain caught at her heart but Lyn said quickly, 'Morgan? About last night. Maybe—maybe you'd rather change your mind.'

Putting a hand over his eyes, he rubbed them to wake himself up and sat up beside her. 'Why do you say that?'

'I've been thinking, about—about my parents.'

'We're not your parents,' he answered on a harsh note.

'No, but—but. . .' She gave him a desperate look, longing for him to tell her that he loved her, but when he didn't said in deep emotional distress, 'Morgan, can I—can I *trust* you?'

It was the only word she could think of, the only one which asked for the assurance that he would never leave her, that he loved her and really wanted to marry her. And on his answer depended so much: whether he would take the opportunity to walk away from his proposal, or if she could put aside forever all these doubts and fears and be happy with him for the rest of her life.

Morgan looked into her anxious face for a moment that seemed to stretch into eternity, then gave a small sigh. 'Yes, Lyn, you can trust me.'

CHAPTER FIVE

'NO, I absolutely refuse to have that woman at my wedding!' Lyn stormed, glaring at Morgan belligerently.

'But your father wants Claire to be there. She is his wife, for heaven's sake.' There was exasperation in Morgan's voice as he tried to argue with her once again.

'I don't care—I don't want her.'

'Look,' Morgan said, trying to be reasonable. 'Your mother is coming and bringing her new husband so why can't you——'

'That's different. *He* didn't break up my parents' marriage. And I very much doubt that my mother loves him. I think she was just trying to prove to Daddy that she's still attractive to other men.'

Realising that they were going round in circles, Morgan tried a new tack. 'Your father's paying for the wedding; he has a right to invite whom he likes.'

'Quite true,' Lyn agreed, her mouth set stubbornly. 'But if he invites Claire then there will be one other person missing from the wedding: the bride! Because if she goes then I don't!'

'That's ridiculous.' Morgan threw himself into a chair. 'Women!'

Immediately Lyn ran to him and sat on his lap, putting her arms round his neck. 'I'm sorry if it annoys you, darling, but please try to see it from my point of view. Think how awkward it will be for me and for my mother if Claire comes. All our friends and relations will be at the wedding, too, you know. But how can we relax and really enjoy the day if she's there, flaunting herself and being possessive over Daddy?' She smiled at him tenderly. 'Perhaps I'm being selfish, but *I* would like to be the centre of attention on my wedding day, not my father's ex-mistress.'

Morgan gave a grunt. 'All right, I understand, and I'll pass on the message, but I'm fed up with being the go-between for your father and you over this.'

Lyn laughed happily. 'I've an idea we'd come to blows if you didn't.' Confident that she'd got her way, she quickly changed the subject. 'Did you sell the lease on your flat?'

'Yes, from the first of October, so I'll have to bring all the stuff I'm not taking away with me round here.'

They went on discussing the arrangements they'd made for the wedding and afterwards. Temporarily, they were going to keep on the flat Lyn had rented until they found somewhere they wanted to live permanently, but Morgan had insisted on taking over the payment of the rent himself. They were to be married on Lyn's twenty-first birthday, at the end of September, only just over two months from the day they'd got engaged. Only a short time, admittedly, but what was there to wait for? Personally, Lyn just longed to make their relationship legal, to seal their romance with the most binding tie of all. She loved Morgan so much that sometimes the intensity of her feelings terrified her, and she was certainly afraid to let him see in case he thought her possessive. But although she tried to hide it and thought she had succeeded, every look she gave him, every time she said his name, she gave herself away.

But she was so happy, on cloud nine hundred and ninety nine, as she told her mother when she phoned her in Australia to break the news. And the weeks since the engagement had been so wonderful: buying the ring, and a whole new wardrobe of clothes for their honeymoon in the West Indies, booking a church and sending out all the invitations. And arranging the reception, most of which she'd had to do herself until her mother flew back to England to take over. It had all been hectic, exciting, and totally wonderful.

And her father seemed to be really pleased, which was an added bonus. Originally, Lyn had been nervous about telling him because she knew her father tended to judge people by their success in life, and she was afraid he would be against someone who had voluntarily given up his career. But greatly to her surprise her father had welcomed her news with whole-hearted pleasure, congratulating Morgan enthusiastically and hugging Lyn. Strangely, he didn't seem at all surprised, and when Lyn remarked on it he laughed and said anyone could see she was in love. Then Jonathan Standish made the offer that lifted Lyn's happiness to an all-time high: he offered to make Morgan a director of his company there and then.

'Why, that's wonderful!' Lyn swung round on Morgan and caught his arm in excitement. 'Isn't that just marvellous?'

She found herself looking into his steady blue gaze and her voice faltered, but then he put a hand over hers and turned to her father. 'Yes, marvellous,' he agreed woodenly. 'Thank you, Jonathan. I hope, though, that you'll give me time off for our honeymoon?'

Her father laughed and waved a benevolent hand. 'Of course. Just come in for a few days a week before the wedding to get the feel of the place.'

So Lyn hadn't seen quite so much of Morgan, but she had been so busy with the wedding preparations that she had no time to feel lonely. Now, just a few days before the ceremony, but when the actual day seemed still an achingly long wait away, she said to him, 'Are all the preparations made for your stag party?'

'Yes—although it seems an outdated tradition,' he added with a grimace.

'Nonsense, you'll love it. I'm just glad that it's a couple of days before the wedding so that you have a chance to recover,' Lyn teased. 'Who have you invited? Anyone I know?'

'Not really. Oh, except Tim Browning; I thought I'd ask him along.'

'Oh, I'm glad you've kept in touch with him; but isn't he at sea?'

'No, he was due for a three-month leave.'

'Have you invited him to the wedding?' Lyn asked. 'It would be nice to have someone there we both know.'

But Morgan shook his head. 'I did suggest it, but it seems Tim's away that weekend.'

Since their engagement Lyn had taken Morgan along to meet most of her relations, but his parents were dead and he'd said he had no one at all close, so the congregation at the church would be made up mostly of their friends and those of Lyn's parents. This saddened Lyn a little; she would have liked to become a part of a whole new family. 'But you must have *some* relations?' she'd pressed him.

Morgan gave her an odd kind of look. 'No one whom you would care to meet.'

His reply intrigued her, and made her wonder if there were some skeletons in the family cupboard, but he had said it so dismissively that she wisely refrained from pushing it any further. For now, anyway—but Lyn made a mental note to find out what he meant while they were on their honeymoon. That, too, she was looking forward to enormously. A friend of her father's was lending them his holiday villa on a small island in the Bahamas for three weeks, although at the moment it was just a hazy kind of dream paradise that wouldn't become reality until after the wedding.

Lyn was wildly happy and Morgan seemed happy enough, too, but she sometimes sensed a kind of wry self-mockery in his manner, which she put down to him having succumbed to matrimony after being a bachelor for so long. At other times, and for no apparent reason, he would become withdrawn, so that she suddenly felt as if he were a cold and aloof stranger, someone she didn't know at all. It frightened her when he did this, and her happiness was so precious that she never dared to ask him why, instead glossing over his withdrawal and pretending that it wasn't happening, putting her trust in the old hope that if you ignored something it would go away.

On the night of Morgan's stag party, Lyn also had

an eventful evening. Her mother had flown to England ahead of her new husband to help organise the wedding, but he arrived that day and Lyn went out to dinner with them. She didn't know what to expect; her mother hadn't spoken all that much about him or his family, although Lyn rightly suspected that this was her fault as she had shown no interest. Beyond knowing his name was Walter Moynihan, shortened to Walt, and that he had three grown-up children and had been a widower, Lyn had only prejudice to guide her. Prejudice that he had caught her mother on the rebound, and a vague idea that all Australian men drank a lot and treated their women as second-class citizens.

Her prejudices received a large jolt as soon as she saw him, for Walt Moynihan was as handsome as her father, more so perhaps in a different, craggier way. He was more open, too, but not at all loud as she'd feared. And he was very evidently in love with her mother, standing up eagerly when she came into the room, making a great fuss of her and generally behaving like a besotted bridegroom. Lyn's eyes widened, and widened even more as she saw the way her mother smiled at Walt and reached out to hold his hand, her eyes full of warm tenderness. So her mother really did love him! Lyn recognised all the symptoms easily enough because she behaved exactly the same way towards Morgan. But did Morgan behave the same way towards her? The flash of doubt was lost beneath the shock of realisation, especially when her mother turned to her and said, 'You didn't believe that I could love anyone except your father, did you?'

Lyn shook her head wonderingly.

'Well, to be honest, I never thought I could, either, but as soon as I met Walt I knew that miracles still did happen after all. We're very happy, Lyn, and we just pray that you and Morgan will be, too.'

That evening gave Lyn a lot to think about, but it also made her feel very sad. In a way she felt that her role and that of her mother had been reversed: it wasn't that her mother was losing a daughter because of Lyn's marriage, but that Lyn had lost her mother because of her marriage to Walt. She would go and live in Australia and become a part of another family's life and Lyn might not see her again, and even if she did they would be virtual strangers. In her heart Lyn had been convinced that her mother had only got married on the rebound and that before too long she would realise her mistake and get a divorce. She had also hoped that her father would come to his senses over Claire, so that her parents could get back together again, but now she had to face the strong possibility that they were parted forever. She had to be pleased for her mother— no one could help but be pleased that happiness had come out of such terrible misery—but Lyn felt a loss almost as great as a bereavement. And because of it her hatred for her father's second wife increased to open bitterness and a desire for revenge. It was an emotion that made her completely obdurate when her father came round to see her the day before the wedding and begged her to let Claire attend.

'No! No way,' Lyn said shortly.

'But she's my *wife*. It's her right to be there with me.' Lyn just looked at him, and his mouth tightened grimly, but he said as persuasively as he could, 'Lyn, please try to see this from my point of view. Claire will feel extremely—put out if she doesn't go. Naturally, she——'

'She's giving you hell, is she?' Lyn interrupted with satisfaction. 'Good!'

Jonathan Standish did a mental count of ten before going on, 'Naturally she wants to be part of our family, to share in all aspects of my life.'

'Well, she isn't going to share in mine.'

'Lyn, all our old friends, people from my company, and a great many business friends are going to be there, and Claire's place is beside me.'

'In other words, she wants to queen it and act the gracious hostess, does she? To usurp Mother's place. But not at *my* wedding!'

Losing his cool, her father said angrily, 'Damn it, Lyn, you're putting me in an impossible position.'

'Damn it, Daddy, you've only yourself to blame,' Lyn shot back, her chin set in an obstinate line.

They glared at each other—a father faced with a daughter who had inherited his own determination of purpose.

'Very well,' he said at length. 'But surely it can't hurt you if she just comes to the reception for a short time. That would be enough to keep her happy and——'

'No.' He drew in his breath in a gasp of scarcely controlled fury. 'I had no idea that you could be so unfeeling.'

'But you should have; after all, I learnt it from an expert,' Lyn retorted tartly.

His face setting, Jonathan Standish said harshly, 'There is no one in the world who would dare to speak to me as you have done.'

Lyn looked at him, her grey eyes shadowing as she realised they were quarrelling again. 'But maybe there's no one in the world who loves you as much as I do, either.'

'Perhaps not,' he agreed more gently. Making a last try, he reached out and covered her hand. 'Please, Lyn, don't be petty about this. Be big enough and strong enough to change your mind. What difference will it make to your happiness with Morgan?'

Lyn looked down at his hand on hers. 'Emotional blackmail, too? She must really be making your life hell.' Slowly she shook her head. 'I wish you hadn't tried that.'

'So nothing will make you change your mind?'

'Sorry, no.'

'You're not sorry, Lyn—you're enjoying this.' He stood up abruptly. 'See you at the wedding, then.'

'You'll still be there? You'll give me away?' she said on a sudden note of panic.

Her father gave her a grim look. 'With pleasure,' he said shortly.

Whatever his inner feelings, her father showed no outward anger when the wedding day came round. The weather was beautiful: a warm, sunny, windless autumn day that was a throwback to summer. They were to be married in London at a fashionable church in Kensington, near Lyn's family home. Morgan had been staying at his flat for the last couple of days and Lyn in hers, but on the morning of the wedding she and her mother drove round to her father's house because he'd wanted her to be married from there. Lyn was a little apprehensive about the idea, but there was no sign of Claire.

The bridesmaids, four of her friends from school, arrived at the house shortly afterwards and there was a lot of excited laughter as they helped each other to get ready. Lyn was in white, of course, in a beautiful brocade dress, and the bridesmaids in pale green. Lyn was almost ready, with just her veil and head-dress to put on, when one of the girls said, 'Don't forget, you must have something old, something new, something borrowed and something blue.'

'But that's so old-fashioned,' Lyn protested.

'Not old-fashioned—traditional,' her mother said firmly. 'Let's see; you have the new dress, of course, and you can borrow this bracelet which is also old, so all you want is something blue.'

'I know, I have a pretty blue handkerchief that should still be in my old room here,' Lyn said, entering into the spirit of it. 'I'll go and get it.'

She slipped out of the guest room they were using and along the corridor to her old bedroom at the back of the house. Somehow she had expected everything to be just as she'd left it when she'd run away to the kibbutz, but all the photographs and pictures had been taken down, and the drawers and wardrobes were empty. Even her books had gone from the shelves. Slowly Lyn walked into the room and looked about her, feeling like a stranger here in the room in which she had spent twenty years of her life. Claire's doing, of course, she thought bitterly. Moving to the window, she looked down at a mark on the window-sill where her favourite ornament had stood, and ran her fingers over it. As she did so a movement outside caught her eye. The house had a small garden and beyond that a mews cottage which was basically a large garage with a servant's flat over the top. Now she saw a woman wearing a cream dress, and a beautiful hat with a finely sweeping feather in the same shade, walk from the house to the garage.

It was Claire. Lyn stiffened, recognising the woman at once, and her heart filed with hatred, but then she made herself relax, refusing to have the day spoilt. Quickly she went back to the others, explaining that she couldn't find the handkerchief, so her mother tied a little bow of blue ribbon at the back of her head-dress instead.

The cars arrived and her mother left, then the bridesmaids. And then it was Lyn's turn. Her father, looking very suave in his morning-suit, escorted her downstairs to have their photograph taken together and then out to the car. He seemed a little subdued, but Lyn was too keyed up to take much notice. The ride to the church was very short. Lyn smiled at the small crowd of people waiting outside to see the bride, and went in from the sunshine to the cool shade of the porch where the bridesmaids were waiting. The procession formed up, but before they moved off Lyn turned to her father, wanting to thank him for everything he'd ever done for her, to make this small moment one they would always remember. She opened her mouth to speak—but he turned his head away and wouldn't meet her eyes.

Lyn stared at him. 'Daddy?' But still he wouldn't look at her.

A terrible suspicion filled Lyn's mind and her eyes swept forward down the body of the church, but she could only see her mother and Walt down in the front pew on her side. The vicar had begun to move slowly down the aisle, the bridal procession following, and her father began to move off, keeping his eyes straight ahead. Puzzled, Lyn fell into step beside him, but her eyes were still searching through the misty softness of her veil. She must have been mistaken, she decided after a few seconds—her father would never play such an underhand trick on her. Relaxed again, her eyes turned to where Morgan was waiting for her at the end of the long aisle, her heart swelling with happiness. And then a long cream plume on a woman's hat swam into her vision behind Morgan's head.

Lyn stopped so suddenly that her father had gone on a pace before he realised and swung a startled face round to look at her. He found himself gazing into grey eyes whose fury was no less muted by the veil. '*How dare you*?' she shot at him. 'Get her out of here.'

'Lyn, please.' He tried to pull her with him. 'Everyone's waiting.'

But, too angry at his deceitfulness to care, Lyn wrenched her arm from his hold and pushed her way through the stunned bridesmaids to the back of the church. One of the ushers was still standing to one side and goggled at her as Lyn swept up to him. Making no attempt to lower her voice, she said, 'You see that woman down near the front on the groom's side, the one with the cream feather in her hat? She's a gatecrasher and I want her removed.'

Her pointing finger was like an accusation and he had no difficulty in seeing who she meant. By now the vicar had realised that the bride was no longer behind him and he came hurrying back. 'What is it? Are you ill? You haven't changed your mind, have you? he asked in dread.

'No. The problem is being dealt with,' Lyn said firmly and gave the usher a push. 'Go on. Get her out.'

The usher walked self-consciously down the aisle as the heads of all the congregation craned round to see what was happening. He passed Lyn's father, who stood still, his face drawn, making no attempt to stop him. When the usher reached Claire it looked for a few minutes as if she was going to refuse to leave. But then Morgan, of all people, turned round and spoke to her and she rose and walked back up the aisle with everyone watching her, her face set into a stony mask. When she reached her husband, Claire said something short and sharp, but he just gave a small shrug and stayed where he was. Her face blazing with anger, Claire continued up the aisle to where Lyn was standing. 'You'll pay for this!' she spat at her, then swept on out of the church.

Lyn took a deep breath, her heart thumping, angry colour still high in her cheeks. For a few seconds longer she stood still, trying to find her former happiness but knowing it was gone. Then she strode down to where her father was waiting and put her hand on an arm that was as rigidly stiff as his face. The procession walked quickly now, past a congregation agog with curiosity, and Lyn gave a small sigh of relief when she reached Morgan. She gave him a quick look of gratitude for having helped to get rid of Claire, but he didn't look at her, merely stepping forward to take his place at her side.

Her voice wasn't very steady when she took her vows, although Morgan's was firm enough, which gave Lyn some comfort. She was beginning to realise the enormity of what she'd done, and was afraid that she had probably alienated her father forever. But that had been a very mean trick that he'd played on her, and she was fiercely glad that she hadn't just meekly let them get away with it rather than cause a scene.

Everyone was very subdued in the vestry when they went to sign the register. Her father was still coldly angry and her mother embarrassed. Lyn turned to Morgan, eagerly expecting him to give her her first married kiss, but his mouth twisted into a grim sort of smile and he merely bent to sign his name.

When they came out of the church there was the photographer waiting again, and they stood in the sunlight in every permutation of groups of family and friends to have more photographs taken. Then they were being pelted with confetti as they got into the car to leave. The reception was being held in a hotel only a short distance from the church, so Lyn knew she had only a little time during the drive when they would be alone. Catching his hand, she said anxiously, 'Morgan, please say you're not angry with me. I *had* to do it. You must see that. I couldn't let her get away with such an underhand trick.'

'Couldn't you?' His face had that withdrawn look that she hated.

For answer she lifted his hand to her face and put her cheek against it, then turned and kissed it. 'I love you,' she told him, her heart in her eyes.

His expression softened and Morgan turned his hand to stroke her cheek. 'Come here, Mrs French,' he said lightly, and bent to kiss her gently on the lips.

Lyn's happiness soared and she forgot all about the nasty incident with Claire. Her father she could win round again—not today, perhaps, but some time in the future—and now all that mattered was that the rest of her wedding day should be as wonderful as she'd hoped.

By the time the last guest had arrived at the reception and had gone down the receiving line, there was no one who didn't know what had happened in the church and why. No one spoke about it, of course, but Lyn got some approving looks from her mother's side of the family and embarrassed ones from nearly everyone who knew her father. But the incident was soon forgotten as the reception continued. Jonathan Standish made a stilted speech and Morgan an extremely good one. He called her his wife several times, which felt wonderful, and she was able to put aside the sudden remembrance that he had never said that he loved her. Tonight, she thought with the supreme confidence that comes with supreme happiness, tonight, when we're alone, he'll tell me that he loves me.

Morgan had booked a room for the night in another hotel outside London, not too far from Heathrow, as they were catching a plane early in the morning. At seven Lyn went up to the room that had been reserved for her to change in. Her mother and a couple of the bridesmaids went with her, but when her mother had made sure that Lyn's going-away outfit was laid out in readiness she went down again, wanting to spend as much time as possible with her relations as she didn't expect to see them again for a long time.

It took a while for Lyn to change because the three of them spent a lot of time going over the wedding, and Lyn had only got as far as taking off the dress and was standing in her long silk slip when the door was opened without a preliminary knock and Claire walked into the room! For a moment they all three stared at her, but, before Lyn could speak, Claire looked at the two bridesmaids and jerked her head towards the open door. 'Get out,' she ordered curtly.

'Look here——' Lyn began angrily.

But Claire said venomously, 'No, *you* look. I have something to say to you that you're not going to like, so I'd advise you to get rid of your friends if you don't want it tittle-tattled all over London.'

Lyn stared at her, on the point of telling Claire to go to hell, but something in the other woman's manner, an aura of menacing confidence perhaps, held her back. Instead she nodded to the other two girls. 'You'd better go,' she said reluctantly. 'But come back shortly; I'm sure this won't take long.'

They left, disappointment at missing another scene obvious in their faces. Claire shut the door behind them and turned the key in the lock, then turned to Lyn with a triumphant sneer on her face. 'It may take longer than you think for what I've got to say.'

'Then perhaps you'd better get on with it,' Lyn said

as coldly and calmly as she could, mentally preparing herself for a tirade of abuse. 'But please remember that I can get you thrown out of here just as easily as I got you thrown out of the church.'

Claire's face sharpened murderously at the reminder, and her eyes swept to the wedding dress where it hung from the wardrobe door, so that for a horrible moment Lyn thought that Claire might try to damage it. But to her surprise the older woman gave a harsh laugh and said, 'You spoilt little bitch! You think yourself so superior, don't you? The happy bride who's hooked her man. Well, if it weren't for me you wouldn't be getting married! And I'll tell you why. Because I picked Morgan for you. I told your father to send him to bring you home, and it was I who said he'd make a suitable husband for a self-centred brat like you.'

Lyn gave a laugh of utter disbelief. 'You're crazy. Do you expect me to listen to such a stupid lot of lies, let alone believe them? You must be——'

'Don't you? Then listen,' Claire cut in. 'I introduced Morgan to Jonathan, and your father paid him to go out to Israel and bring you back. And when it became obvious that you were still too pig-headed to accept his marriage to me, it seemed that the best thing was to marry you off. And as you were making such a lovesick fool of yourself over Morgan I suggested to your father that he ask Morgan to marry you. Morgan refused, of course,' Claire said viciously. 'Who wouldn't! But your father, for some inexplicable reason, feels that he owes you something and wants you to be happy, so he offered to pay Morgan to marry

you.' Lyn gasped and Claire smiled at her like a
spitting cat. 'He had to pay a very high price, of course,
but then, he'd have to to get a spoilt brat like you off
our backs.'

'You're mad!' Lyn broke in angrily. 'Really mad!
Morgan and I love each other.'

Claire gave another of her mocking laughs. 'If you
believe that, then I can only say that Morgan must be
a superb actor. You may love him, but he *certainly*
doesn't love you.'

Lyn glared at her furiously, wanting to tell her how
wrong she was but held back by the knowledge that
Morgan had never told her that he loved her, and
knowing that the denial would never ring true. A
triumphant look came into Claire's eyes. 'Don't you
want to know how much your father had to pay him
before Morgan would take you on?'

'You're lying,' Lyn said tightly.

Ignoring her, Claire said, 'The price was a
directorship in your father's company, a flat in
London, and——' she deliberately paused for a
moment '—a quarter of a million pounds. Half to be
paid to Morgan today, and half in six months' time.'

Jerked into sudden action, Lyn strode over to her.
'You're lying,' she said again. 'You've made up the
whole pack of lies to try and hurt me because you
wanted to get back at me for not letting you get away
with your dirty trick in trying to sneak into the church.
Well, you tried and you failed, so now get out of here
before I call the manager and have you thrown out.'

But Claire stood her ground. 'You're such a child
you won't even accept the truth. Truth that I can

prove,' she added with a victorious sneer.

'All right, prove your lies,' Lyn challenged. '*If* you can.'

'Oh, I can, quite easily.' Claire smiled, taking her time, letting the doubt fester. 'I know that your father offered to buy Morgan for you because I was there while he did so.'

'If you call your word proof——' Lyn said on a derisive laugh.

'Oh, but I don't. All you have to do is look in the pocket of Morgan's jacket—there you will find a cheque from your father for one hundred and twenty-five thousand pounds.' She spelt the words out slowly, letting them sink in. 'An extremely high price for someone who Morgan says is hopeless in bed.'

Lyn's face whitened in shocked fury and she took a step towards Claire, her hand raised.

'Don't you *dare* strike me!' her tormentor rasped. Slowly Lyn lowered her hand, her face still ashen. Turning to the door with the key in her hand, Claire smiled again, knowing that she had won. 'And while you're about it,' she said scathingly, 'why don't you ask Morgan why I was sitting on *his* side of the church?' Putting the key in the lock, she turned it, gave Lyn a last smile of pure contempt, and finally left.

The bridesmaids must have been waiting right outside the door because they came in immediately after Claire had gone. They found Lyn standing in the middle of the room, staring into space, and had to speak to her twice before she blinked and looked at them. 'Are you all right, Lyn?'

'What? Oh—yes, of course. I'm fine.' She managed

a travesty of a smile. 'I must finish getting changed. Morgan will be waiting.'

Catching her change of mood, the three of them didn't talk very much now as Lyn quickly changed into her going-away outfit. And soon she was ready, looking very chic in a pale grey suit with red accessories. Instead of going back to the reception with the bridesmaids, Lyn said in a strained voice, 'Would you find Morgan for me and ask him to come up here for a moment, please?'

There was a fitted wardrobe on the wall facing the door, with a full-length mirror. Lyn stood in front of it as she waited, but not seeing herself at all, instead searching inwardly into her memory, desperately searching for something that would prove Claire wrong.

Morgan came very quickly. He knocked and entered the room when she answered. Lyn didn't turn when he came in but looked at him in the mirror. He, too, had changed and was wearing a dark suit. Somehow he always looked taller and slimmer in a suit. Her eyes flew to his face, looking for any signs of wariness, but it seemed that he didn't know about Claire's confrontation. His gaze met Lyn's in the mirror quite openly and he gave a lazy smile. Coming up behind her, Morgan put his hands on her waist and lightly kissed her hair. 'You look very lovely,' he said in a voice that certainly sounded sincere, even to Lyn's straining ears.

'Thank you.' She put her hands over his and leaned back a little, her eyes fixed on his reflection.

'Why did you want to see me?' he asked when she

didn't speak at once.

'There was something I wanted to ask you.'

She felt his hands stiffen for a second and then relax as he said, 'Well?'

'Claire was sitting just behind you in the church; didn't you realise she was there?'

He didn't take the way out she offered him, and instead the withdrawn look came into his face. 'Yes. I did.'

'You knew I didn't want her there,' Lyn said, trying to keep her voice level. 'Why didn't you tell her to go before I arrived?' He was silent and her heart contracted. Slowly, painfully, she asked the question that Claire had told her to ask. 'Why was she sitting on *your* side of the church rather than next to my father's place?'

His fingers tightened on her waist, but Morgan made no attempt to avoid the issue, his eyes still on hers in the mirror. 'Claire is my cousin,' he said shortly. 'It was she who introduced me to your father.'

She stared at him, a curious roaring sound in her ears, and yet she could hear perfectly clearly. 'Why didn't you tell me?'

'You were so against her that I knew you wouldn't come back to England on the boat with me if I did.'

'And it was important that I come back on the boat with you?'

His brows flickered. 'Yes.'

It felt as if time had stopped, that the world stood still. Lyn dragged her eyes from his image in the mirror and turned to face him, feeling as if her body were lead and that everything was in slow-motion. He still held her by the waist, and lifting her hands she put them on his chest, one hand over the pocket of his jacket. He had a flower in his buttonhole, a yellow rose-bud from her bridal bouquet that she'd given him earlier. Lyn bent to smell it but it had no scent. She pressed her hand against his pocket but could feel nothing inside through the smooth material. Looking up into his eyes, she made one last desperate plea. 'Morgan?' But he said nothing, his face set into lines of stony expectancy, and with a sob she plunged her hand into his pocket and took out the piece of folded paper she found inside. It was a cheque for one hundred and twenty-five thousand pounds and signed by her father.

Lyn made a strangled sound in her throat and stepped away from him, unable to bear his touch.

'Who told you?' he said heavily.

'*Who the hell do you think*?'

'Claire came here'

'*Yes*. She told me everything. Everything! She rammed it all down my throat and showed me what a —what a sham I've been living, believing.' Lyn's voice broke and tears came into her eyes, but fury came to her rescue and she thrust the cheque back into Morgan's pocket. 'Here! Take your hard-earned money. Only I'm sorry, but you won't be collecting the next instalment because I never want to see you again.' Striding past him she pulled open the door. 'Now get out of here! Go on. *Just get away from me.*'

CHAPTER SIX

PULLING the door from her hand, Morgan thrust it shut and turned the key, locking Lyn in with an enemy for the second time that day. 'You've heard Claire's side; now you can hear mine.'

Lyn laughed in his face, the tears of rage wet on her cheeks. 'Your side! You just mean more lies and deceit.'

'No, I mean the truth, all of it,' Morgan answered grimly.

'*No way.* I never want to hear you or see you again, so just get out of here. Go away!'

'I'm not going anywhere until you've heard what I have to day,' Morgan told her forcefully. 'And then we're both going together—on our honeymoon.'

'Honeymoon? Lord, you must think I'm dumb if you think I'm ever again going to believe a word you say. Not that I intend to listen.'

Lyn turned on her heel and headed for the bathroom but Morgan strode forward and caught her arm. 'Oh, no, you're not going anywhere until you've listened to me. You owe me that much.'

'Owe you?' Lyn swung round to face him in an absolute fury. 'I don't owe you anything—*you've been paid*!'

Morgan's face tightened at the scathing derision in her tone, but his jaw thrust forward belligerently. 'I was going to tear up that cheque as soon as I had the opportunity. I'd already told your father that I didn't want it.'

'Shut up!' Lyn pulled her arm free and covered her ears. 'You're lying again. You're just afraid you're going to lose the other half of the payment if you don't live with me for six months. You rotten swine! You pig!' Turning suddenly she ran for the phone beside the bed and grabbed up the receiver. 'This is room 406,' she yelled. 'Send a security man up at once. There's an intru——'

Her words were broken off as Morgan grabbed the phone from her. 'Sorry, it was just a joke,' he said into it as he held Lyn off. 'My wife has had a little too much to drink.' He put the phone down and jerked his head back as Lyn lashed out at him. Catching her arms he gritted angrily, 'You little wildcat. Will you keep still and listen?'

For answer she began to kick him, giving a triumphant yell when he winced. Morgan pushed her away and held her at arm's length. Lyn struggled wildly but her skirt was too tight for her to reach him. Her hair, which she had done up in a pleat for the wedding, came loose and fell down about her shoulders but she didn't even notice. Panting, she became still at last, but the eyes she raised to Morgan were full of hurt anguish, momentarily buried beneath a greater rage. 'I hate you!' she yelled at him. 'Do you hear me? *I hate you. I hate you. I hate you.*'

Her voice rose to a scream but Morgan suddenly jerked her forward, his face white and grim. 'I told you you could trust me. And I meant it. I haven't——'

'No! I won't listen.' Lyn began to scream again but

he shook her, then let go one of her arms to put his hand over her mouth. Immediately she scratched his face, her nails raking down his cheek.

Morgan cursed forcefully, saw his face in the mirror and swore again. 'You hellcat! There's only one thing to do with you.' Carrying her over to the bed, he dropped her on to it face down and sat astride her, his hand on her head, almost smothering her in the pillow.

Lyn tried to buck him off and beat furiously with her fists, her yells of rage muffled in the softness. Dimly she heard him speaking on the phone but was too murderously angry to hear what he said. Belatedly it occurred to her to go limp and pretend that she'd fainted, but Morgan didn't fall for the ruse, holding her where she was for some little time until a knock came at the door. Then he suddenly jerked her to her feet, pulled her into his arms and kissed her after saying, 'Come in.'

She tried to push him away, as infuriated by his kiss as she was desperate to see who had come into the room, but Morgan held her so tightly, one of his hands in her hair, that she couldn't even move her head. All she could see was that his eyes were open and he was watching someone behind her. As suddenly as he'd pulled her up Morgan drew away, turning her round to face the door but twisting one of her arms up behind her back. 'Follow them,' he commanded curtly, and she saw that two of the hotel porters were carrying her luggage out of the room.

'No, I damn well—ouch!' She gasped as Morgan twisted her arm.

'And smile,' he said fiercely into her ear. 'We're going on our honeymoon.'

The corridor outside was empty and as soon as they reached the lift Morgan kissed her again so that she couldn't speak, much to the amusement of the grinning porters. Keeping a tight hold on her arm, he almost ran her through a side entrance to where a taxi was already waiting, and bundled her into it. Lyn made a dive for the other door but he caught her and pulled her roughly back, holding her head against his shoulder so that she couldn't scream. He didn't let her go until they were well away from the hotel, and even then kept a firm grip on her arm.

Gasping for air, her hair a dishevelled mess and black smudges around her eyes where her mascara had run, Lyn nevertheless came up fighting. Throwing herself forward, she tried to attract the attention of the driver, but the glass panel between them had been closed. She went to open it but stopped and turned when she heard Morgan laugh behind her. 'He won't take any notice of you,' she said shortly. 'I told him that you're drunk—just as I told the porters.'

'Well, he'll soon find out that I'm not!' Lyn flashed back.

'Look at yourself,' Morgan said sardonically. 'And then see whether he'll believe you or not.'

She stared at him, sitting there with such grim determination in his face. A face that an hour ago she had loved more than any other in the world, and now hated and despised. He was so strong, both mentally and physically. Lyn felt an overwhelming sense of helpless frustration at her own weakness. She put up a trembling hand to touch her hair and suddenly all the fight went out of her. She was filled with an all-consuming sense of loss, an emotion akin to deep, painful grief, for this shattered love. Tears pricked at her eyes and she turned away from him, fighting to control her emotions so that he wouldn't see her cry.

'Lyn?'

She shook him off and leaned back against the seat, her hands balled into tight fists and pressed hard against her temples, her body trembling. The taxi rattled on through the heavy London traffic, stopping in jams and at crossing lights, but Lyn made no attempt to try to get out—Morgan's hand still gripped her arm and she knew he wouldn't let go. But it didn't really matter; he couldn't hold on to her forever, and she would soon be free of him. The sooner this farce of a marriage was over the better.

She sat slumped in the corner of the seat until the taxi turned on to the motorway and began to go faster, then Morgan said brusquely, 'Here, take my handkerchief. Clean yourself up. We'll be at the hotel soon.'

Slowly Lyn lowered her hands. She thought of refusing because she really didn't care how she looked, but pride came to her rescue and she took the crisp white handkerchief Morgan held out to her, being careful not to look at him. There was no mirror in which to see herself in the taxi and her bag had been left behind at the reception hotel, but she scrubbed at her eyes and combed her hair with her fingers. Having made the effort, she unthinkingly picked up the handkerchief and began to nervously twist it in her hands as she sat back in the corner again and stared out of the window.

The hotel that Morgan had chosen for the first night

of their honeymoon was an elegant Georgian country
house a few miles from the motorway. The taxi pulled
up outside and Morgan helped her out, giving her a
wary glance as he let go of her to pay the driver. But
Lyn made no attempt now to escape from him, instead
standing woodenly beside him as she waited, her face
set into a controlled mask, only her grey eyes showing
the pain and desolation of her inner feelings. He
escorted her inside and signed the register. 'Mr and
Mrs Morgan French' she saw him write. How
wonderful she had thought that sounded before this
afternoon. Putting his hand under her elbow again,
they followed the porter up the beautiful wide
staircase to a room on the first floor.

Lyn didn't even look at the room; while Morgan was
tipping the porter she walked across it and into the
bathroom, bolting the door behind her. There was a pretty
frilled stool in the corner. Lyn sat on it and leaned against
the wall. The shock of what had happened hit her now
and she trembled convulsively. Her head ached
unbearably and waves of dizziness came and went. It was
as if the physical shock of it had been held in check until
this moment when she was at last alone.

'Lyn?' Morgan rapped sharply on the door. 'Lyn?
Are you all right?'

'Go to hell!' she answered weakly, and got up to
hang on to the basin as she tried to fight off a growing
feeling of nausea—a battle that she lost. Afterwards
she slumped down on the floor, her head against the
coolness of the tiles.

She must have sat there for a long time, enveloped
in a kind of mental numbness, because the sun had

gone from the room when Morgan again knocked on
the door. 'You've been in there long enough, Lyn.
Come on out.' She didn't answer and he said angrily,
'If you don't open the door I'll break the damn thing
down!'

She believed him; she believed now that he was
capable of anything. Getting hold of the basin to pull
herself up, Lyn stared at her swimming reflection in the
mirror. How different! How grotesquely different she
looked from this morning. She had a sudden desire to
laugh hysterically but it came out as a sob. Her hand
trembling, she turned on the tap and washed her face, but
the dark, bruising shadows round her eyes were of
unhappiness now and wouldn't wash off. She dried
herself and took a last look in the mirror, consciously
bracing herself as she pushed back the bolt and walked
into the bedroom.

Morgan was leaning against the wall by the
bathroom door. He had taken off his jacket and tie and
turned back the cuffs of his shirt. He looked big and
tough and menacing. Lyn gave him only a passing
glance and went across to the window, looking out
over well-kept grounds to the distant aurora of orange
light that hung over London. Coming up behind her,
Morgan put his hand on her shoulder and said, 'Lyn,
we have to——'

'*Don't touch me!*' Her eyes suddenly blazed at him
from her ashen face.

Slowly he lowered his hand. 'We have to talk,' he
said shortly.

She looked at him malevolently for a moment, then
nodded. 'Yes, we do.' She saw his eyes lighten and

added coldly, 'But don't think that I'm going to listen to your so-called explanation, because I'm not. The only thing I want to discuss is how quickly that—that mockery of a marriage ceremony can be annulled.'

'It doesn't have to be annulled,' Morgan said earnestly. 'If you would only hear me out you'd know that I married you because that's what I wanted—very much.'

'Of course you did,' Lyn said in a grimly sardonic voice. 'You *very much wanted* a quarter of a million pounds, not to mention a flat in London and a directorship of Daddy's company.' Turning away she looked round the room for the first time. It was dominated by a large four-poster bed. And the room was full of flowers. A fit bower for a wedding night, she thought wretchedly. There was even a bottle of champagne standing in a bucket of now-melted ice. Going over to it, she took out the bottle and tore off the foil.

'Let me do it for you.'

Morgan came to take it from her but she turned her back on him and did it herself, twisting off the cork and watching the golden, bubbling liquid as it frothed out of the bottle. Then she picked up one of the two glasses from the tray, filled it, drank it down in one swallow, and filled it again.

'Getting tight isn't going to help,' Morgan pointed out caustically.

'It's my wedding night,' Lyn answered in bitter irony. 'I'm entitled to have a drink.' A dreadful thought occurred to her and she couldn't stop herself inflicting the masochistic pain of voicing it. 'Or did you order it for yourself? To fortify you against the unwelcome ordeal of having to go to bed with me?'

His blue eyes gazed at her intently as Morgan said, 'And what exactly does that mean?'

'Oh, please don't go on pretending.' Lyn gave a derisive, unsteady laugh. 'It hardly matters now, does it? Because she told me that, too, you see, your precious cousin. About the little chat you'd had when you told her how naïve and boring you found me in bed!'

'Lyn, that isn't true.' Morgan came quickly to her side and reached out for her. 'I wanted you from the first moment I saw you and——' His words were suddenly cut off as Lyn, unable to bear to hear him lie on this subject above all others, threw the contents of her glass in his face.

Her eyes were glacier-cold as she walked over and refilled her glass, but her voice was quite calm when Lyn said, 'I apologise; that was a waste of good champagne.'

His jaw taut as he fought to control himself, Morgan took out a handkerchief and wiped his face, and his voice was far from steady as he said tersely, 'How can you possibly believe Claire after the weeks we've spent together? You *know* how wonderful I found you in bed, how I've—I've gloried in making love to you.'

'I thought I knew,' Lyn agreed. 'But now I don't care any more.'

'Don't you?' Morgan took a determined step towards her as if to try and prove her wrong.

Quickly Lyn stepped back, away from him. 'If you touch me again I'll scream the place down,' she threatened, the high note of near hysteria in her voice stopping him short in his stride.

They stared at each other, each realising they had reached an impasse. It was Morgan who moved first. Lifting his hand, he pushed his hair back from his forehead in a fed-up gesture. 'This is futile,' he said shortly. Then, with a sigh, 'Lyn, I'm sorry. I know this has been a hell of a day for you. Look, why don't we go down and have dinner? Maybe you'll feel better when you've had something to eat, and we'll be able to sit down and talk this thing through rationally.'

'No.'

'No to what?'

'No to everything. I don't want to have dinner with you. I don't want to talk about it. As far as I'm concerned, it's over.'

Morgan's mouth set into a bleak line. 'In other words, you'd rather take the word of Claire, a woman you hate and whom you've made hate you, rather than that of the man you loved enough to marry—and who cared about you enough to marry you,' he added steadily, his eyes on her face.

Her own eyes filled with pain. 'Don't you dare say that now. I've always known in my heart that you didn't really love me. What that sadistic bitch said today only proves it.'

He looked at her for long seconds and she could see by his taut jawline and his clenched fists that he was struggling to control himself. Then Morgan swung abruptly away, thrusting his hands into his pockets. He stood with his back to her for several minutes before turning to face her again. Lyn was momentarily shocked by the bleakness in his eyes. The money must mean a lot to him, she thought in wretched misery, if it hurts him that much to lose it.

'There's no point in trying to talk to you when you feel like this,' he said eventually. He ran a hand over his face, over the still livid scratch-marks on his cheek. 'OK, if I promise not to try to talk to you about what's happened, will you come down and have dinner?'

'No.' An infuriated look came into his eyes but faded when Lyn added, 'I—I can't. I can't face anyone.'

'No one here knows,' Morgan pointed out.

'They know we're supposed to be on our honeymoon,' Lyn said bitterly. 'Why else did they leave the champagne and the flowers?' Her eyes came up to meet his, full of hurt and hate. 'And right now I don't feel like a newly-wed.'

'All right, so I'll ask them to bring dinner to us here.'

'Don't you listen? I don't want to have dinner with you,' Lyn said tartly, the anger breaking through again. 'I just want to go home. I want to be done with this!'

'Home?'

'To my flat.'

'Our flat,' he corrected her. 'The place where we're going to live after we get back from our honeymoon.' Her eyes widened at the implication, but he lifted his hand in a negative gesture. 'Forget that for now.' Going to the phone, he rang down and ordered dinner.

Lyn went and sat in an armchair by the window, leaning back against the padded seat. She felt deathly tired, as if all her strength had drained away. But she would need her strength if she was going to fight Morgan. She saw now that he had no intention of letting her go. He was going to try and keep up this travesty of a marriage to get the rest of the money her father had promised him. He would try and persuade her that it was all lies, of course; he'd started that already, and she was quite sure that he would use every means in his power to try to win her round. Her glance flicked to the big four-poster bed and Lyn felt a hot blush of shame as she remembered just how willingly she had given herself to him—and how expert a lover he was. If he ever got her in that situation again she knew that it would take all her resolve to resist his arguments, to resist him. So she must make sure that she got right away from him so that the opportunity never arose.

Coming across to her, Morgan sat on the edge of the bed. She gave him a morose look but he reached out and took her hand, refusing to release it when she tried to pull away. 'It's all right,' he said soothingly and began to stroke the back of her hand. His voice gentle, he said, 'Poor Lyn, you've had a hell of a day. I'll never forgive Claire for ruining it for us.' He felt her hand stiffen at the hated name, but went on, 'What we need now is time. Time to get over the shock of this and start thinking clearly again.'

'My head is quite clear,' Lyn interrupted sharply.

'Is it? I doubt it. In the circumstances it's a wonder you haven't broken down completely.' He paused and his hand tightened on hers as he looked earnestly into her face. 'It was to prevent that that I had to use such rough and ready tactics on you. I'm sorry, darling. I hope I didn't hurt you, but I *had* to get you away from the reception.'

'Of course you did,' Lyn said icily. 'How else were you to prevent me from going down and asking my father to confirm the truth?'

'Not the truth.' Morgan shook his head. 'Just Claire's version of it.'

'Her version sounds right to me—she told me the cheque was in your pocket!' Lyn flashed, snatching her hand away.

Getting to his feet, Morgan walked over to where he had hung his jacket on a trouser press, took the cheque from the breast pocket and walked over to her. Standing in front of Lyn, he held the cheque so that she could see it and deliberately tore it in half, then into quarters and tiny pieces. 'I wanted to do this when your father insisted on putting it in my pocket,' he told her, 'but tearing up a wedding present cheque I'd just been given would have looked odd at the reception, and I had no chance to do it before I saw you.'

'Some wedding present,' Lyn said sarcastically. Standing up, she pushed past him as she said, 'I don't want to hear.'

'But if you won't listen, how the hell are we supposed to sort this thing out?' Morgan demanded, his anger with difficulty held in check.

'There's nothing to sort out,' she answered as steadily as she could. 'It's over. Finished. Tonight we go our separate ways and we'll have the wedding annulled as soon as possible. Unfortunately for you, you won't get your directorship, or your flat, or the money, but you know who to blame for that, don't you?'

Morgan gave her a hard, sardonic look. 'It isn't that easy. We've already been to bed together so there's no question of an annulment.'

She stared at him, momentarily thrown by the certainty in his tone. 'But I thought a marriage had to be consummated. . .' She bit her lip. 'It doesn't matter,

I'll get a divorce instead.'

His brow drawing into a frown, Morgan said firmly, 'I'm not going to let you rush into any hasty actions, Lyn. We're going to go to the West Indies so that you have a chance to think straight and——'

'You're crazy!' Lyn said on a note that was close to hysteria again. 'It doesn't matter what you say; I'm not going anywhere with you. Now or ever.'

'Do you really want everyone to know what's happened, then?' Morgan said sharply. 'I left word at the wedding reception that we'd decided to sneak away, but everyone will know that your marriage has broken up before it started if you go back to London. Even the media will be interested in a marriage that lasted only a few hours—the tabloids will hound you until they milk you dry.'

Lyn stared at him, her face even paler than before. 'Better to be hounded than to spend another hour with you!' she answered bravely. But although she defied him, the thought of what he'd described filled her with horror. And that it would be known, she was sure. If Claire didn't leak the story out of spite then Morgan certainly would out of revenge.

'You'd do much better to go away with me as if nothing had happened,' Morgan argued. 'That way no one can hurt you.'

'Except you,' she pointed out bitterly.

'I've never wanted to hurt you, Lyn.'

He said it so steadily, his eyes holding hers that one could almost have believed him. 'Don't you call deceiving me, marrying me for money, hurting me?' Lyn retorted.

'I didn't marry you for money, and the only thing I've deceived you in is by not telling you that Claire is my cousin. Otherwise everything I've ever said to you, I've meant.'

Remembering what he *hadn't* said, her eyes filled with pain. Morgan frowned when he saw it and reached out a hand, but she walked away. Not that there was far to walk; the room suddenly seemed like a cage, and the big four-poster bed a cage within a cage. Everything felt oppressive, as if the room was crowding in on her, and she longed to be free, to go outside into the open air and run and run until her strength gave out. Turning blindly, she lunged for the door, her hand reaching out for the brass knob. But Morgan reached her before she could turn it and pulled her back.

'No, please let me go.' She struggled feebly in his hold. 'I feel so ill. Must get some fresh air.'

'There's no point in trying to fool me,' Morgan started to say harshly, but then gave an exclamation as her legs buckled and she slumped against him. 'Lyn?'

She didn't answer so Morgan picked her up and carried her to the bed, laid her on it and stood looking down at her, his blue eyes concerned, his brows drawn into a deep frown. He made no attempt to bring her round but after a while Lyn stirred and opened her eyes. Seeing him standing over her she gave him a heavy-lidded smile. But then memory came flooding back and her face filled with desolation. Without saying anything, Lyn turned her face away from him and was still lying there when two waiters brought their dinner to the room.

Morgan opened the door and gestured towards a small table. 'Over there will do.'

'Would you like us to stay and serve you, sir?'

'Thank you, no. We'll serve ourselves.'

'Very good, sir. Oh, and the manager's compliments and this parcel was sent over for the lady.'

'Thank you.' Morgan took the plastic shopping bag that was held out and closed the door behind them, then came over to stand beside the bed. 'Come on, Lyn you'll feel better when you've eaten. This came for you.'

'What is it?' she asked dully, sitting up.

Morgan opened it and brought out the handbag she'd left behind at the reception. And inside it, of course, was her passport. So now even that excuse for not going with him to the West Indies had been taken from her. Lyn felt a great weight of inevitability settling on her shoulders, a weight so leaden she had no strength to shake it off.

Putting his hand on her arm, Morgan helped her up and led her over to the table where he sat her in a chair as if she were a child and could do nothing for herself. She didn't want to eat anything, but Morgan lifted the lid of one of the dishes, allowing the rich smell into the room, and her poor stomach let her know how empty it was.

'I don't know about you, but I didn't get round to eating very much at the reception,' Morgan remarked in a voice so matter-of-fact that nothing might have happened. He ladled some soup into bowls and sat opposite her. Lyn gave him a baleful look, hesitated, then picked up her spoon and began to eat.

He was right—she did feel better afterwards. Lyn

sat back when she'd had enough and put her napkin on the table. Her brain was beginning to function again and she realised that not only her passport had been returned with her handbag, but also her money and credit cards. Now she could go downstairs, order a taxi, and get away from this terrible situation. But it was as if Morgan could read her mind. He was sitting with a glass of wine in his hand, watching her. His mouth thinning, he said, 'Don't even bother to think about it, Lyn. I'm not going to let you go anywhere without me until this is sorted out. And I know you're going to take a lot of convincing before you even start to believe me, so I'm afraid you have no alternative but to go to the West Indies.'

'You can't make me,' Lyn said on a new note of defiance.

'Possibly not,' he agreed, to her surprise. 'But the only way you're ever going to stop me taking you with me is by creating a hell of a scene at the airport. Is that what you really want?'

'It might well be preferable.'

'Even if I agreed that the trip would be on your terms?'

'What do you mean?'

Morgan shrugged. 'Exactly that. You lay down the ground rules. We talk when you're ready to talk. And you don't have to listen until you feel you want to hear what I have to say.'

'And—and the sleeping arrangements? Lyn asked guardedly.

He gave a short, bitter laugh. 'Whatever you say.'

Her lips had gone dry and Lyn put out the tip of her

tongue to lick them, unaware of the way Morgan's hands suddenly clenched. She tried hard to think through the woolliness that seemed to clog her brain. Going anywhere with Morgan now would be like a self-inflicted punishment, but if she went back to her flat Claire was bound to find out and let everyone know that the marriage was already on the rocks. It would be one shame to add to the other, and Lyn wasn't sure that she could take any more. So why go to the flat or with Morgan? She had her passport and could go anywhere she wanted. But the same thing still applied, she realised, only this time it would be Morgan who would tell everyone. Again that heavy feeling came over her and she greatly envied the ostrich. Right now, she would be extremely grateful to let the world go on without her.

Lifting her head, she said on a sharp, frightened note, 'And tonight?'

'Our wedding night?' Morgan's voice, too, didn't sound very steady. 'I suppose you'd better take the bed and I'll have the armchair.'

She looked at him for a long moment, wondering if she could trust him, then gave a high inner laugh that shrieked in her brain. Of course she couldn't trust him. That was what this whole thing was about, wasn't it? The fact that he'd lied and cheated—for money. But if he thought he might yet sweet-talk her round, then perhaps he would keep his word, for now. Lyn sighed, realising that it was the easiest of all the evil options, and the only one that would give her some kind of dignity when she came back to England and left him for good. 'All right,' she said slowly. 'I'll go with you tomorrow.'

Morgan's tense face immediately relaxed and he smiled. 'Good girl,' he said approvingly.

Devastated by the smile, Lyn pushed her chair back and stood up.

'I'm very tired. I'm going to bed.'

'OK. I'll put the trays outside.'

Picking up her overnight case, Lyn went into the bathroom to shower and change, but when she opened the case found that she had only the beautiful cream silk and lace nightdress to put on. It had been bought specially for tonight, of course, and was low-cut and clinging, moulding her body and enhancing all the curves that Morgan loved to caress. No—that she'd thought he loved to caress. Now? Now she didn't know, would never know. All the youthful pride in her own body, all the awakening belief in her power to attract, had gone, had been trampled underfoot in the mud and dirt of his betrayal.

She changed quickly, trying not to think of how this night should have been. She brushed her hair without looking in the mirror, not wanting to see herself, trying desperately not to care. Unbolting the door, Lyn walked out into the bedroom and saw that Morgan had turned off the main lights and the room was lit only by the soft glow of the bedside lamps. She stood for a moment, looking very young and vulnerable with her unmade-up face and bare feet.

Morgan was sitting in the armchair, waiting, but he got slowly to his feet, his eyes going over her and his body stiffening. 'Lyn.' He said her name on a harsh, unsteady note and held out his hand towards her—but Lyn ignored him, walking past as if he weren't there and going round to the other side of the bed, getting quickly into it and turning off the lamp.

For a few moments the tension in the room was electric, but then Morgan swung round and went into the bathroom. Lyn let out her held breath in a long sigh, but lay tensely in the big bed waiting for him to come back. When he did, Morgan came over to the bed and looked down as she lay with her back to him, her body rigid. 'Do you mind if I take a pillow and a blanket?' he asked with heavy irony.

She shook her head wordlessly and heard him settle himself in the armchair. Then the light went out. Lyn was glad of the darkness but she couldn't relax. She was much too aware of Morgan for that. She would have given a great deal to be alone, to be able to cry out her hurt, to give way to this agony of pain and humiliation. But pride held her stubbornly silent, her taut nerves listening for any sound or movement from Morgan, ready to fight him off if he made the slightest advance. But he was as still as she, although Lyn knew intuitively that he was awake, his thoughts probably as preoccupied as hers. And probably thinking along the same lines, she realised: he must be cursing Claire for spoiling his plans as much as Lyn was. Maybe I ought to be grateful to her for telling me the truth, Lyn thought wretchedly. But then knew with sudden fierce decision that even to have lived a lie with Morgan would have been better than this.

A clock somewhere in the hotel chimed every hour and half-hour; Lyn lay and listened to it for a long time but eventually fell into an uneasy sleep. The phone ringing with their early morning call woke her, and she turned to find that Morgan was in bed beside her!

He answered the phone and turned to look into her furious, hate-filled grey eyes. Before she could speak, he said shortly, 'The armchair was damned uncomfortable, and you didn't even know I was here.'

'You made a promise,' Lyn began indignantly, but then her eyes grew scornful as she gave him a shrivelling glance. 'But I should have known that someone as despicable as you would never keep his word!'

'If you were a man I'd knock your head off for that,' Morgan said angrily. He got up and Lyn saw that he had been lying on top of the blankets with just the top spread over him. It was too late to apologise, not that Lyn would have done anyway. All the hurt came pouring back, but Morgan had deliberately left their call to the last minute so that they had to hurry to pack and have breakfast before they left for the airport, and there was no time to dwell on it.

Lyn didn't eat very much and there were dark shadows round her eyes. She looked a different person from the rapturously happy girl of twenty-four hours ago. Morgan gave her several frowning glances in the taxi as she sat in a bleak, withdrawn silence, but when they reached the airport she walked resignedly alongside him to the check-in desk. They handed in their cases and went to turn away, when Lyn became aware that Morgan had stopped, his body stiffening. Looking past him, she saw Claire standing near by. Lyn gasped, but Morgan put a warning hand on her arm.

'You're up very early,' he said guardedly to Claire.

'I thought I'd come and see you off,' Claire

answered, her eyes fixed with satisfaction on Lyn's stricken face.

'Really?' Morgan said sardonically. 'Well, now you've seen us.'

He went to move on, but Claire, her eyes still fixed on Lyn, said, 'My dear, how wretched you look! Didn't you get much sleep last night, I wonder? Perhaps you have something on your mind.'

Lyn's eyes blazed, but it was Morgan who spoke. Putting his arm round Lyn's shoulders in a protective gesture, he said, 'Last night was our wedding night. What the hell else did you expect than that we would look tired?' And, keeping his arm round her, he led Lyn towards the departure lounge, leaving Claire looking after them with startled uncertainty in her face.

The touch of his hand burned through her clothes and as soon as they were out of sight Lyn broke free from Morgan's hold. 'She came to see whether or not we caught the plane,' she said bleakly, realising how quickly and spitefully Claire would have spread the news if Lyn had stuck to her first decision and refused to go.

'Yes.'

Morgan's answer was so short that she realised he was angry too. Lyn glanced up at him, wondering just how close his relationship was with Claire. They were cousins, of course, but that could mean anything. Not all cousins were close. But Claire had introduced Morgan to her father and, according to her, it had been her idea that he should go to Israel and bring Lyn home. And Claire had also said that it had been at her instigation that Jonathan Standish had paid Morgan to marry Lyn. She had said it was to get Lyn off their backs, but was it also to help Morgan? If so, she had completely blown it now, so it was no wonder that Morgan was angry.

In the departure lounge Morgan found a couple of seats, but Lyn just dropped her things on to hers and walked over to the huge windows, watching the planes take off and land in quick succession. She could still feel the weight of Morgan's hand on her shoulder, and she was filled with shame that she hadn't instantly shaken it off. His gesture had allowed her to retain a little pride in front of Claire, even though it had been a pretence. But it also made her feel that now she owed him something, which only added to her humiliation at his hands. Biting her lip, Lyn stared up at the sky, her hands clenched. She didn't want ever to owe Morgan anything. She just wanted to go on hating him as much as she did now.

Another big jet took off and she heard their flight called. Soon they would be winging their way into the sky, too, to spend three weeks of what should have been the start of a wonderful future together. Now the time stretched ahead as an ordeal that hung over her like a prison sentence. But she would be the only prisoner and Morgan her unrelenting gaoler.

CHAPTER SEVEN

DESPITE its name, the island of Grand Jabalya in the Caribbean was too small to have an airport, so Lyn and Morgan had to fly to the nearest international airport at St Vincent and then take a seaplane. It was a new experience for Lyn, and ordinarily she would have enjoyed seeing the great spray of water that came up from the floats as the plane zoomed across the harbour, until the sea reluctantly let it go and it rose into the sky. She glanced back and saw that they had left behind a wake that reminded her vividly of the *British Bounty*. But the memories that evoked were too painful, too full of deceit to contemplate, and Lyn turned away from the window, her face betraying her feelings for a few wretched moments before she managed to recover the cold mask again.

Morgan was sitting beside her, his shoulders too wide for the seat in this much smaller plane. He was looking past her as he, too, took in the view from the window, but his sharp glance told her that he had seen the mask slip. I must be more careful, Lyn told herself in bitter determination. I won't let him see how much he's hurt me. I won't! Because pride was all that was left. That and hate. She clung to those strong, surface emotions like a person on the edge of a black hole, afraid to let go of them in case she was sucked into some deeper hell.

The flight to Grand Jabalya took less than an hour,

but there was the car, a red convertible that Morgan hired from England, to be collected, and then the drive to the bungalow. 'Here.' As they left the quayside Morgan passed her the map and directions they'd been given. 'Guide me through the town, will you?'

'Guide yourself,' she returned shortly, and thrust the map back at him.

His mouth tightened. 'Behaving like a sulky schoolgirl isn't going to do any good, Lyn.'

'Don't you like it?' she asked tauntingly. 'Such a shame. But then, they say that people get what they deserve.'

Morgan gave her a grim look, but stopped to study the map before driving on. The traffic drove on the left-hand side of the road, the same as in the UK, but the cars were all American with the steering wheel on the left instead of the right, which took some getting used to. It might have been petty, but Lyn felt a morbid satisfaction when Morgan took the wrong turning and had to go back. But he only did it once, and then they were out of the sprawling main town and driving along a coast road cut out of the side of a mountain with a sheer drop to the sea on the other side. The road went through a curving rock tunnel and came out to a spectacular view of a wide bay, the sea an unbelievable blue, the hills green and lush, and the sun shining hotly from a cloudless sky.

The perfect setting for a honeymoon, Lyn thought with masochistic irony, and put up a hand to shield her tired eyes from the sun.

The villa was on the other side of the bay, down a track leading from the main road, a cool, white

one-storeyed building in the midst of a garden that was
ablaze with flowering plants and trees, their colours
so rich and exotic that Lyn could hardly believe they
were real. Morgan drew up outside and they both sat
for a few minutes, taking in the beauty of the house
and its setting. It was perfect, exactly the right
hideaway for two people in love. The thought filled
Lyn with an overwhelming sadness, and she again put
her hand up to her eyes.

'You OK?' Morgan asked brusquely.

'The sun is so strong.'

'Don't you have any sunglasses?'

'I think I packed them. I——' Lyn broke off abruptly
as she realised that to cover up her own weakness she was
having an almost normal conversation with him. Turning
away, she got out of the car.

'We have to collect the keys from the next-door
house,' Morgan reminded her as he followed her out.
'According to the instructions it's about half a mile
away. I could do with stretching my legs. Want to walk
along with me?'

'I told you—I don't want to go anywhere with you,'
Lyn answered scathingly, and walked round the
bungalow and down into the garden. There was a
terrace at the back of the house with a metal table and
chairs, and below that a swimming pool with built-in
seats against the side so that you could sit in the water
and have a drink. But it was the garden that drew Lyn
like a bee to honey. Red, orange and mauve
bougainvillaea climbed everywhere it could get a
hold, and hibiscus bushes edged a stone path that
meandered through flower-filled terraces shaded by

fronded palm trees until the soil gave way to sand and
Lyn walked out on to a beach that stretched in a great
white crescent round the bay. A beach of dazzling
white sand that was completely deserted.

Impulsively, she kicked off her shoes and pulled off
her tights, then walked across the beach to the sea. The
waves licked at her toes, the nails of which had been
painted a pretty coral colour especially for her
honeymoon. It was the first time that Lyn had really
been alone since the wedding. As she looked down at
her toes the tears suddenly began to fall
uncontrollably. Her body shook with sobs so great that
her chest hurt and she put her hands across herself in
a futile attempt to try to contain them. Swaying as if
she'd had too much to drink, Lyn staggered a few steps
and dropped on to her knees, the waves soon soaking
her skirt. Putting her head in her hands, she cried out
the shock of hurt and despair until there were no tears
left, only dry, racking sobs that made her ribs ache.

Slowly Lyn became aware of her surroundings
again. Some time must have passed because the tide
had gone out and she was no longer kneeling in the
sea, and the sky had begun to turn red as the sun sank
towards the horizon. Pushing herself up, she walked
down towards the sea and scooped up some water to
wash her face. She didn't feel any better—just
drained. But it had been necessary, that outburst of
grief for a lost love; it had acted as a catharsis, leaving
her temporarily empty of all emotion.

Turning, Lyn started to wander along the beach, her
feet making deep footprints in the wet sand that were
filled by the next rippling wave. As far as she could

see there were no other houses along the bay, although there were a couple of fishing boats pulled up on to the beach further along. She hadn't expected the bungalow to be as remote as this; she and Morgan would be virtually alone. Her foot touched something hard and she bent down to scrape away the sand from a half-buried shell. It was large and beautiful, the inside edge a deep, pearly pink colour. Lifting the shell to her ear, Lyn could hear an echo of the waves at her feet. Her eyes drifted to the deep golden blaze of the sunset, but then her skin prickled, warning her that there was someone nearby. Quickly she swung round. Morgan was a few paces behind her, changed from his suit into casual shorts and T-shirt, his bare feet making no sound on the soft sand. It was the way he had always dressed on board the *British Bounty*, the way he'd looked when Lyn had fallen in love with him. For a moment her heart jolted and she wanted to run to him and be held in his arms again, to wake up and find that this whole thing was some terrible nightmare.

Her fingers tightened on the shell until the sharp edges dug into her flesh, the pain forcing her back to the wretchedness of reality.

'What have you found?' Morgan asked. 'It looks like a conch shell.'

He came to stand beside her and put out a hand to touch the shell, but Lyn whirled round and sent it flying as far out to sea as she could throw. It landed with a splash and sank quickly back into the water. Then she turned and looked at Morgan with defiant eyes, daring him to make any comment.

His lips twisted a little, but he judged her mood

accurately enough and merely said, 'I'm going to prepare a meal; come along if you're hungry.'

Without waiting for her to answer, Morgan casually turned away and walked back along the beach. Lyn watched him, determined not to do anything he suggested, but the sun was very low in the sky now and the palm trees cast dark, unnerving shadows across the shore. She shivered, suddenly feeling cold, her damp skirt clinging to her legs. Morgan was out of sight now, had disappeared among the palms at the foot of the hills. Afraid that she might not find the path to the bungalow in the dark, Lyn hurried after him, following his footsteps.

As it was, she found the path easily enough because Morgan had turned on the lights in the house. Glass doors leading to the terrace stood invitingly open. Lyn walked up to them and paused, not wanting to go inside but knowing there was no alternative. It took quite an effort of will to step through the doors into the large sitting-room beyond. The walls were painted stark white, but there were so many other bright, ethnic colours in the room, in the settees and carpets and pictures, that you hardly noticed the plain walls. Turning to close the windows behind her, Lyn's eye was caught by the last of the sunset and she stood still, fascinated by the primeval beauty of the evening sky.

The sound of a door opening made her glance round as Morgan came into the room. Quickly she looked away but was aware of him as he came to join her at the window. He didn't speak, just stood beside her as he, too, watched the sunset, but when the sun at last slipped below the horizon, Morgan stirred and said,

'That was quite something. I don't think I've ever seen such a marvellous sunset—not even when we were on the ship,' he added with emphasis.

Deliberately Morgan brought her mind back to that time, little knowing he had no need to do so. Lyn turned and found herself looking into his keen blue eyes. Glancing down, he said, 'Your skirt is wet.' He grinned. 'And you seem to have forgotten your shoes.'

Realising that she'd left them on the beach, Lyn said flatly, 'I'll get them tomorrow.'

Moving away from him, she walked out of the room into the wide corridor. Opening off it on the right there was a big kitchen with a breakfast bar, and on the left a large bedroom with a bathroom and a smaller bedroom with a shower-room. In the second bedroom Morgan's pyjamas were laid out on the bed and his toilet things were in the shower-room. And in the main bedroom all Lyn's clothes had also been unpacked and her nightdress laid out on the coverlet in the sexy way the maids did it in high-class hotels.

Lyn took one look and went storming back into the sitting-room. 'How dare you touch my things?' she blazed. 'You keep your filthy hands away from them!'

Morgan gave her a startled look, but then his face tightened as he said shortly, 'Why the hell shouldn't I touch them? After all, I've touched every part of *you*.'

She stood there staring at him, completely thrown by his remark, her eyes wide with shock. 'You have no right,' she stammered. 'It doesn't give you the right to—to. . .'

'We were close, Lyn,' Morgan said intently. 'No two people could have been closer than we were.'

He lifted his hand to touch her arm but Lyn stepped away from him. 'No,' she said bitterly. 'You wouldn't even have looked at me if I hadn't had a rich father. His money was the only thing you wanted to get close to.'

'That isn't true,' Morgan denied forcefully. 'Listen, I——'

But Lyn broke in and said, 'No, you listen, for once. The only reason I'm here is to give the lie to any rumours your precious cousin might spread about us. I have no intention of listening to your so-called explanations, so don't try it. In fact, don't talk to me at all, because I certainly shan't be talking to you!'

'Do you know what you sound like?' Morgan answered exasperatedly. 'Like a child who's suddenly realised that the world doesn't revolve round her, and who can't face up to——'

Slamming the door behind her, Lyn strode out of the room and went into the main bedroom. She shut that door hard, too, but when she looked was dismayed to find that the door didn't have a lock. She gazed at it in perplexity, then carried a chair over and tried to wedge it under the handle as she'd seen it done it films. Only somehow it didn't seem to work so well in real life. Lyn was quite sure that if Morgan really wanted to come in after her he wouldn't have any difficulty at all in doing so. She stood back worriedly, but after a few moments took the chair away. What the hell was she afraid of? Now that Morgan's deviousness had been exposed, going to bed with her was the last thing he wanted. After all, he'd only done it to get her to marry him in the first place, and had probably hated every minute of it. He must have just closed his eyes and thought of all the money that was coming his way, Lyn thought on a growing wave of hysteria.

Fighting for self-control, she lay for a long time in a hot tub, then changed into a pair of pyjamas. The nightdress that Morgan had laid out on the bed she bundled up and threw into the rubbish bin; from now on sexy nightdresses were no longer part of her life. Just as sexy men would never again have a part in it, Lyn resolved fiercely. When she was free of Morgan she was going to make darn sure that no one else ever had the power to hurt her.

It was dark outside now, although she wasn't sure what the time was because she hadn't bothered to adjust her watch. Jet lag didn't help, of course, but strangely she didn't feel particularly tired although her stomach was giving her urgent messages for a refill. But food was out in the kitchen, which meant facing Morgan. So what? she told herself. She had to eat.

Pushing her hair back from her face, Lyn went out into the kitchen. She had considered the nightdress to be sexy and didn't realise how the silk of the pyjamas clung tantalisingly to her firm young figure, outlining it at one moment and hiding it the next. And she looked so young and unspoilt with her bare feet and loose hair.

Morgan looked round from the steak he was grilling, his eyes going over her before he turned back to his task, his mouth set into a grim line. He didn't attempt to speak to her and she went over to the fridge to see what there was to eat. To her surprise it was quite full. There were bread, eggs, ham—all the usual things, as well as several more exotic fruits and vegetables that she didn't recognise. Whoever looked after the house while the owner was away must have provided the food, she supposed. Hunger overcame her and Lyn made herself a big ham and tomato sandwich.

'There's coffee in the pot, if you want some,' Morgan told her.

She hesitated, but then said, 'Thanks,' and poured out a large mug.

Morgan had finished cooking his steak and carried it over to the breakfast bar. 'Are you going to be adult enough to join me?' he asked drily.

Without bothering to answer, Lyn put the sandwich and mug on to a tray and carried it into her bedroom.

Sleep was difficult that night. Lyn went to bed after she'd eaten but lay awake for a long time, listening to the unusual silence of the night: no traffic noises as in London, no engines and pounding waves as on the ship. Here there was only the occasional cry of a night-bird and the soft swishing sound of waves rippling on the beach. The only man-made noises were those made by Morgan as he cleared up after his meal, then turned on the radio in the sitting-room, and an hour or so later his door closing as he went into his own room. Lyn listened tensely to those sounds, and only slowly relaxed when she was certain that he had gone to bed. She tried to plan then, to sort out what she was going to do with her life, but it was too soon, the hurt still too raw, and all she could think of before she finally fell into an exhausted sleep was how gullible and foolish she'd been.

Jet lag played havoc with her body clock and it was

gone noon when Lyn woke the next day, but even though she'd slept so long she felt heavy and lethargic and couldn't be bothered to get up. Anyway, what was the point? What was there to get up for, except to spend more long hours in the close company of the man she hated? But Lyn wasn't slothful by nature and the sunlight round the edges of the curtains beckoned. Getting up, she put on a bikini, opened the french windows that gave on to the terrace where Morgan was sitting, and crossed it to dive straight into the pool.

He lowered the magazine he was reading in surprise, and watched as Lyn swam round the pool half a dozen times in a burst of energy. Her strength spent, she floated on her back for a while, but the sun was too strong so she climbed out by the steps. Lifting her hands to wring the water from her hair, Lyn stood at the edge of the pool, her body outlined against the sun, her stance unknowingly provocative. Morgan was sitting on a soft-mattressed lounger and had put out another alongside his. It was much too close; after getting herself some fruit juice from the fridge Lyn pulled the lounger a good yard from Morgan's before sitting down on it.

His mouth twisted sardonically but Morgan merely said, 'I hope you slept well.' She didn't answer and his voice hardened. 'Are you going to pretend that I don't exist?'

She gave him a contemptuous glare. 'I wish you didn't exist. I wish I'd never met you.'

'But you did, and things happened that can't be changed.'

He went to go on but Lyn said quickly, 'No, but the

future can be changed and I intend to make sure that it does—and as soon as possible.'

Morgan gave her a sombre look. 'Be careful you don't make the biggest mistake in your life.'

She gave a harsh, bitter laugh. 'Oh, I already made that!' Draining her glass, she set it down on the ground, then pushed her wet hair back behind her ears, not caring what she looked like because she knew that Morgan had never really cared. And with fastidiousness also went modesty and mystery. Morgan didn't want her, so what the hell did it matter? Lyn unclasped her bikini top and tossed it aside, revealing the soft mounds of her breasts, silky pale against the rest of her tanned body.

Leaning back she closed her eyes, but opened them again when Morgan said tightly, 'Is that for my benefit? Or is it supposed to be some kind of punishment?'

She gave him a surprised look. 'Neither. I did it because I want to sunbathe this way. As you only ever took me to bed to further your own ends, I don't see why it should have any effect on you.'

'Aren't you rather young to be so masochistic?' His voice changing he said urgently, 'I always wanted you, Lyn. I wanted you every time we made love——' he paused and added with heavy deliberation '—and I want you *now*.'

Lyn didn't answer, just gave a cold, disbelieving smile and closed her eyes again.

Reaching out, Morgan took hold of her wrist. 'Lyn, I know you're upset and angry, but just try and think things through, will you? Remember how things were between us on the ship. Do you really think that the way I made love to you then could possibly have been a pretence? No man could have——'

'Shut up!' Lyn tore her arm from his grip and jumped to her feet. 'You're a cheat and a liar and nothing you say will ever convince me otherwise.' Running into the bungalow she found a long T-shirt and pulled it on, then went through the garden and down to the beach. Turning to the left, she walked in the shallows until she reached the point of the bay where rocks that had fallen from the cliff face blocked the way. She clambered up on to one of them and spent the next hour watching the crabs in the rock pools as the tide went out.

Morgan had followed her down as far as the beach, but when he saw that she was settled on her rock he went straight into the sea for a swim. He was a good swimmer, his powerful arms propelling him through the waves until he was quite a long way out to sea. Lyn watched him under her lashes until it suddenly occurred to her that these were Caribbean waters and that there might be sharks out there. Fear ran through her and she began to get to her feet to call him back—but then remembered and hesitated. She sat down again, overcome by this betrayal of her emotions and put her hand in her mouth, biting hard on her thumb, uncertain what to do. But Morgan turned almost immediately and swam safely back towards the shore. Lyn gave a sigh of relief, as much because she hadn't given her feelings away, feelings that she was ashamed of herself for still having.

When she went back to the bungalow Morgan

wasn't around, so Lyn took off the shirt and sunbathed again, dozing a little, letting the sun soothe her mind to a comforting emptiness.

'Aren't you hungry?'

Morgan's shadow was standing over her as Lyn reluctantly opened her eyes. 'When I want something I'll get it,' she answered acidly.

'How about driving into town for meal tonight?'

'With you? *No way.*'

'What a little coward you are, Lyn,' Morgan said on a note of contempt. 'I really thought you'd have had more guts then to let Claire's poison get to you like this.'

'The only time I need guts is right now—to resist *your* poison!' she retorted.

He glared down at her in baffled anger. 'Just how long is it going to take before you snap out of this?'

'Forever, hopefully.'

He swore, and turning on his heel strode into the house where he must have tried to lose his anger in music, judging from the loud rendering of the *1812 Overture* that soon came flooding from the sitting-room. Lyn listened for a while, then slipped into the pool again and swam until she was too tired to do another stroke.

That evening, Lyn waited until Morgan had eaten before she went into the kitchen to fix herself something, but when she went to take the tray into her bedroom Morgan stood up and barred her way.

'Oh, no, you don't. We may be a world apart emotionally at the moment, but I'm not going to let you run away into a corner and hide all the time, Lyn. If you're going to eat, then you can eat here at the table like a civilised human being.'

'And if I refuse?' she demanded, her chin raised antagonistically.

'Then I'll *make* you damn well sit here,' Morgan answered, his jaw thrust forward with equal forcefulness.

She stared at him, for a moment glimpsing the anger and strength that simmered beneath his surface control. A *frisson* of fear ran down Lyn's spine as she realised how physically superior he was to her and how easily he could make her do what he wanted. Maybe it would be a mistake to push him too far. Her lashes flickered. 'All right, you don't have to do your Rambo act.'

Carrying the tray over to the table, Lyn sat down and picked up her fork. Morgan looked at her for a moment then turned away with an angry, exasperated gesture. Shoving his hands into his pockets, he went out on to the terrace and stood looking bleakly down across the garden to the sea, his body taut as he strove to control himself.

Lyn didn't attempt to eat. His outburst had shaken her, although it shouldn't have done; after all, he had used strong-arm tactics to get her out of the wedding reception hotel. But somehow that had been different. There had been a note almost of desperation in his voice just now. But she instinctively knew that Morgan had recognised it, too, and was angry with himself as much as with her. She stole a look at him, realising that although she was alone here with him it had never even occurred to her before that he might harm her in some way, might try and force her to do what he wanted. There had always been the instinctive feeling that she would be safe in his hands. Even when he had lied to her and deceived her, she had been willing to come here with him because it had never entered her head that he might physically harm her. And she didn't think that now, not really. Morgan would have to be pushed far over the edge before he became defeated enough to lose control.

Lyn frowned, her food forgotten as she tried to push emotion aside and to think rationally. It just didn't add up. Surely he would have to be desperate for money to marry someone he didn't love. OK, he didn't have a steady job, but he had willingly given up his career for a while to . . . Lyn's eyes widened. Unless he had lied about that, too. Of course, that must be it! He hadn't left his job of his own accord—he had been fired like the others when the stock market collapsed. According to Claire, she remembered, his price had included a directorship of her father's company, which would not only give him a job but also re-establish his status in the City.

Bitter distaste filled her throat and Lyn pushed her plate away, her appetite gone.

'So you're refusing to eat now, are you, you little fool? Putting on a big martyr act, I suppose.'

Morgan was standing at the french windows, looking at her derisively. Crossing over to the drinks tray, Lyn poured herself a large drink from the nearest bottle, her hand trembling.

'I told you before: drink isn't going to help,' he told her harshly.

He took a threatening step towards her, lifting his

hand as if to take away the glass, but stopped short
when Lyn glared at him, her grey eyes flashing fire.
'No, it won't, but at least it will help to get rid of the
foul taste you leave in my mouth!' And she swung
away and strode to her room.

For the next few days they kept a wary distance
from each other, like wild animals respecting each
other's territory. If she had been alone, this remote
house and its setting would have been an ideal place
for Lyn to lick her wounds, but with Morgan
constantly there the tension could only heighten. And
perhaps it increased for him, too, because Lyn became
every day more aware of his growing impatience with
the situation. It wasn't helped by there being no other
people and nothing to do except sit around in the sun.
There was nothing else for Lyn to think about, and she
found it almost impossible to plan for the future when
Morgan was always there. His tall, powerful body in
just a pair of swimming trunks, wet from the pool, was
a deadly distraction that made her quickly close her
eyes, her chest tight and her hands balled into tight
fists of frustrated need.

In a spirit of bitter defiance she continued to
sunbathe and swim topless, convinced that Morgan
couldn't care less. And whenever he tried to talk to her
she turned on him, snapping at him to shut up and leave
her alone. He stood it a couple of times, but at the third
his face grew so angry that Lyn was afraid he would
retaliate in some way. Instead, he strode out to the car
and drove away in the direction of the town.

It had been dark for some time when he came back,
hours later. Lyn had long since decided that he had

gone out drinking and had defiantly had a few herself. She was in her room, her ears straining for the noise of the car, but her emotions were very mixed when she finally heard it. Morgan made no attempt to be quiet as he came into the house. He was whistling some tune she didn't recognise and came and banged on her door.

'Hey, you coming for a swim?'

'No. Go away!' she called out angrily.

'Suit yourself.'

Lyn heard him go into his room and after a few moments come out again, presumably to go through to the pool. She wondered what he'd been doing to make him sound so cheerful. Having a good time somewhere, meeting people, she supposed, and felt irrationally jealous. She listened for him to come in again but there was no sound for a long time and she grew restless. If he'd had a lot to drink he might have got cramp or something while he was swimming. He might have drowned. Don't be ridiculous! she admonished herself, and tried to go to sleep. But after another few minutes Lyn pushed the cover aside and ran out to the terrace.

Only the underwater lights were on, giving the water a strange, luminous look, like a deep pool in a cave. For a few minutes Lyn couldn't see him and she ran round the edge calling, 'Morgan!' in a high, frightened voice.

'I'm here.' He was floating on his back in the deep shadow of a tree, but turned and swam quickly over to her. 'What is it?'

'Oh, I. . .' She felt utterly stupid. 'It's nothing.'

She turned to go back in but Morgan had pushed

himself up out of the water to stand beside her. He was quite naked.

'For heaven's sake!' Lyn exclaimed in outrage. 'Must you—flaunt yourself?'

'I'm sorry,' Morgan answered sharply, but caught her arm as she went to go past him. 'I didn't think I was going to have the honour of your company,' he reminded her on a sarcastic note. Then, more gently, 'What is it, Lyn? You sounded frightened when you called me.'

'I told you, nothing.' She tried to pull away from him agitatedly. The silk of her pyjama sleeve was already wet where he had got hold of her and drops of water had splashed on to her, making the material transparent.

'There must have been something to send you out here,' Morgan persisted. Adding wryly, 'The way you've been behaving since we got here, I can't see you willingly coming anywhere near me.'

'There wasn't. It was—it was a mistake.' Again she tried to pull free. 'Let go of me, can't you? Do you think I *want* to look at you in that state?'

'Why, what difference does it make when you say you don't care about me any more? After all, *you* do it all the time and it isn't supposed to affect me.' His grip tightened as she began to struggle. 'Or maybe you're not as immune to me as you make out.'

'Let me go!'

Lyn hit out at him but Morgan put his arms round her. 'Let's find out, shall we?' Holding her pinned tightly against his chest, he bent and kissed her.

His mouth was possessive, demanding, and so

achingly familiar that for a moment Lyn could only stand transfixed by memories, the old hunger rushing through her veins. Her heart began to pound and she made a small moaning sound against his mouth. 'Lyn.' Morgan said her name on a deeply urgent note. His kiss became even more passionate and he held her closer until she felt the growing tension in his body. Lyn knew that she must break free, that she mustn't let this go on. She tried to struggle but her own body betrayed her, its inner compulsion melting her will-power and leaving her pliant in his arms.

Lifting his head, Morgan gazed down at her for a moment with hope and growing hunger in his eyes. The firm roundness of her breasts showed clearly through the wet pyjama jacket and he lifted his hand to brush his fingers across them, making the nipples rise and harden. Lyn cried out and a great shudder ran through her. His eyes darkening with need, Morgan arched her towards him and bent to kiss her breasts through the silk.

The eroticism of it devastated her senses. To feel his lips, his tongue, so close and yet not have them actually touch her, drove her mad with frustration. Her breath grew hot and panting and Lyn put her hands on his shoulders, her nails digging into him. When she began to feel that she could stand it no longer, Morgan lifted his head to kiss her throat, his lips burning a pattern of desire on her hot skin. His hands went to the buttons of her jacket, pulling them open, fumbling in his hurry. She writhed as he fondled her, her hips moving against his until he groaned aloud. Suddenly he pulled her close to him, his hands low on her waist, making her feel the hardness of his body. 'Now you know how much I want you. Don't you? Don't you?' he demanded, his voice thick and unsteady.

'Yes, I. . .' Lyn gave a long moaning sigh. 'Oh, yes.'

'And you want me just as much. You can't deny it, not any more.'

Lyn didn't try—her body moving against his gave its own voluptuous answer. With a cry of animal triumph, Morgan lifted her into his arms and carried her towards the house.

Twining her arms round his neck, Lyn kissed his ear, biting the lobe as he hurried towards the house and her bedroom. He groaned and muttered something under his breath. Lyn smiled, remembering the first time he had carried her to bed. But then they had been at sea during the storm and the floor had pitched beneath his feet. She remembered how eager she had been, how she had longed for that moment she had begun to think would never come, and the fear in her heart in case he hadn't wanted her.

The memory went through her mind like a lightning bolt. Lyn gave a great gasp and jerked free of his hold, pushing him away from her as she did so. Caught off balance, Morgan stumbled against the wall. He reached for her again, but stopped precipitately when Lyn screamed out, 'No! No!' She ran for her room and slammed the door but Morgan immediately flung it open, sending her flying to the floor. He grabbed her before she could get up and hauled her to her feet. 'What the hell——?'

'No! Let me go. I don't want you. I don't! I don't!' Lyn's voice rose in fear and anger. 'Oh, you devil. You trickster.'

Morgan shook her roughly. 'There was no trickery,' he said in a fury of disappointment. 'You were doing what you wanted to do. Nobody made you.'

'No!' Lyn broke away from him, knowing that he was speaking the truth but in anguish that her body had betrayed her so.

'What was it, then—just a big tease?' Morgan demanded roughly. 'Were you just trying to see if you could turn me on? Was that what all this going around topless was leading up to?'

He waved a contemptuous hand towards her breasts and Lyn hastily grabbed a towel to cover herself but Morgan jerked it angrily away.

'OK, so you proved your point,' he rasped. 'And now you can damn well follow through.'

Shaking her head in alarm, Lyn backed away as he strode towards her. 'I wasn't teasing. I didn't mean to——' She broke off as she reached the wall and looked up into his dark, menacing face.

'Like hell you weren't' Morgan lifted his head, his throat taut as he strove to control himself, his hands gripped into white-knuckled fists. There was sweat on his face and a pulse throbbed in his temple. After a few moments he said in cutting coldness, 'It's all right, you don't have to be afraid. I don't force myself on women—even my wife. Although I have an idea that's what you want. Because you're as hungry as I am, although you can't bring yourself to admit it.'

He turned and went to the door, but when he reached it looked back with a contemptuous glance and said, 'And I don't beg, either—especially from my wife!'

CHAPTER EIGHT

THEY left the island the next morning. Lyn hadn't slept at all and by seven was packed and ready to leave, but there was no phone at the bungalow and the keys to the car were in Morgan's room, otherwise she would have taken it and to hell with him. As it was, she went into the kitchen to make herself a coffee and waited until he got up an hour or so later.

He paused in the doorway when he saw her, his eyes growing cynical as they took in the skirt and jacket she was wearing. 'Running away?' he said drily.

'I'm leaving, if that's what you mean,' Lyn answered as coolly as she could.

'As I said: running away.' Going over to the table, Morgan poured himself a mug of black coffee and leaned against the sink to drink it. He was wearing just denim shorts and a T-shirt, his legs bare.

'I never wanted to come here in the first place,' Lyn reminded him. 'It was a mistake. I shouldn't have listened to you.' She glanced at him and then looked quickly away, remembering last night and cursing her own weakness.

Morgan gave a harsh laugh. 'When did you ever listen to anything except your own selfish ego? The trouble with you, Lyn, is that you're eaten up by jealousy.'

She stood up in anger. 'I don't have to listen to your opinions. You're just being spiteful, anyway. Give me the car keys and I'll go.'

Slamming down his coffee mug, Morgan lunged forward and pushed her back into her seat. 'No—for once in your life you're going to shut up and listen.' Holding her firmly, he went on, 'You were so jealous of your father falling in love with Claire that you did everything you could to break them up, even going so far as to run away. You didn't really care that he'd fallen out of love with your mother—you just couldn't take the fact that he loved someone more than you!'

'That isn't true!' Lyn exclaimed hotly. 'I——'

'I said shut up and listen,' Morgan repeated forcefully, thrusting her back into the chair. 'And that's why you refused to let Claire come to the wedding and made that scene at the church—you were pushing your father to choose you instead of her. But you made sure it was on a day when he had no real choice at all. You couldn't even play fair on that! I bet you even hoped that it would break them up, even though you knew your father was happy in his new marriage. You didn't really care about him. All you really wanted was to be the centre of his attention again.'

Lyn's cheeks flushed with anger. 'You don't know what you're talking about,' she said acidly. 'And if you think I'm going to take any more of this, then——'

'Then you'd be right,' Morgan finished for her. 'You've shut yourself up in a shell and refused to listen to me from the moment Claire talked to you after the wedding, but now you're going to hear what I have to say whether you like it or not.'

'No!' Lyn put her hands over her ears, but they were

ruthlessly pulled down. 'I'll scream,' she threatened. 'I won't listen to your lies!'

Morgan looked at her in disgust. 'You selfish little coward. I don't know what the hell I ever saw in you to make me fall in love with you.'

Suddenly still, Lyn stared at him, the colour draining from her face, then she gave a bitter laugh that was almost a sob. 'Oh, you really shouldn't have said that. I still had some respect left for you because it was the only lie you never told —until now. You never once said that you loved me.'

His eyelids flickered but Morgan said grimly, 'I've never lied to you. *And I'm not lying now.* I didn't want to have the bother of bringing you back from Israel when your father suggested it, especially after Claire told me what a spoilt little brat you were. They'd known where you were all along, incidentally, but they'd decided to let you cool your heels in the kibbutz in the hope that it might teach you some sense. Not that their hopes stood any chance,' he added sarcastically. Lyn shot him a fuming glance but he went on, 'Then something happened and your father decided that he wanted you to come home, so he——'

'What happened?'

Morgan hesitated, then said heavily, 'I can't tell you that, although I'd like to. But I promised him I wouldn't and I'm not going to go back on my word, even though it might knock some sense into your silly little head.' He looked at her coldly. 'As I said, I didn't want to bring you back, but then I saw a photograph of you and I changed my mind.'

Lyn looked at him sharply at that and the acid remark

she had been about to make died on her lips. Her body was still tense but she didn't push against his hold and sat silently as he continued, 'But something your father said just as I was leaving made me realise that he wanted to see you married and that I was a candidate for the role. So I decided that when I collected you I would put you on a plane and return alone with the car—but then I met you and I changed my mind yet again. I decided that I wanted to know you better.' He paused and then said shortly, almost as if against his will, 'I didn't fall in love with you at first sight, if that's what you're thinking. But I admit I was attracted to you. And I thought that Claire had done you an injustice, that you couldn't be that selfish.' His mouth twisted as he gave a sardonic laugh. 'Which just shows you how wrong you can be.'

'You don't have to tell me any more,' Lyn said shortly. 'I know the rest. Your greed overcame all these fine principles and you married me for the money my father offered you,' she said with acid bitterness.

'Not everyone is as selfish as you, Lyn,' Morgan returned harshly. 'I knew that your father would be pleased to see me marry you, and that's one of the reasons why I fought against it. I wanted to make my own decisions. Marriage was an option—something to think about if we got along OK. But I fell in love with you on that voyage—deeply in love. And the day that I took you to bed was the day that I decided to marry you. But I wanted to do it in my own time and on my terms, not with your father pushing me.'

'Do you really expect me to believe this?' Lyn asked in a tight voice.

'I don't give a damn whether you do or not; we're

through anyway, but you're going to hear it all before we leave here.' He paused, gathering his thoughts, then went on, 'When we got back to England it was obvious to your father that what he wanted had happened and we were in love. He wanted me to marry you at once, but I wanted time to convince you that we could have a good life together without my taking up my career in the City again. I didn't want to go back to that kind of life. I'd seen what it could do to men - and to their marriages. But you and he had the fixed idea that to be a king rat in the rat race was the only way to live.' His eyes settled on her face. 'So, because I loved you so much and I wanted you to be happy, I put my own wishes aside and accepted your father's offer of a place in his company. I also agreed to let him give us the flat because he insisted that he was going to give it to you as a birthday present anyway. The money I wasn't prepared to take, and he knew it, but he went ahead and put the cheque in my pocket at the reception. He's as stubborn as you are,' he added bleakly.

Lyn's eyes were wide and vulnerable, betraying a mixture of emotions. Incredulously she said, 'It can't be that simple. If it were you would have told me at the time.'

'There was really nothing to tell, just a clash of wills between me and your father which I gave in to because——' Morgan broke off, but added quickly, 'It was your making Claire hate you so violently that pushed her into remembering the offer your father had made me and twisting it in such a way that she could use it to try to turn you against me. Which it did,' he said bitterly. 'And with results that were even more fatal than she expected. She wanted to hurt you, but she didn't want to break us up.'

'How can you possibly know that?'

'Because she wouldn't want to do anything that would hurt your father.'

'You mean, she was careful not to do anything that would make him see through her before,' Lyn said shortly. 'But when I tell him about this——'

'You won't tell him,' Morgan cut in curtly.

'And why not?' she bristled.

'Because Claire is pregnant, that's why not. That's right,' he sneered, looking at her stricken face. 'You're going to have a baby brother or sister. And pregnant women, especially older women who have been badly upset, sometimes do crazy things. And that's what your father will believe because it's what *I'll* tell him. That Claire was so upset that she twisted a few facts into a story that no one in their right mind would have believed.' Leaning forward, he said forcefully, 'I'm not going to let you hurt Claire any further and I'm not going to let you hurt your father, either. You've done enough damage.' Then he straightened up. 'I'll pack and be ready to leave in ten minutes.'

The news of Claire's pregnancy had so thrown Lyn that she could think of little else until they reached the harbour. Her thoughts were chaotic, but as she went over what Morgan had told her two questions began to burn into her brain. A sea plane was leaving for St Vincent almost immediately, but because they only got on at the last minute they had to sit apart. It gave Lyn another chance to think, and she determined to ask

Morgan the two vital questions as soon as they got on the plane to England. But when they reached St Vincent airport Morgan went up to the reservations desk to change their tickets and came back with only one in his hand.

'They've got you on to the next flight to London. It leaves in a couple of hours.'

Lyn frowned. 'But what about you? If there isn't enough room for both of us then I don't mind waiting until——'

'I'm not going with you,' Morgan broke in shortly.

'But...' Lyn stared at him, recalling how he'd said they were through. 'But you *must*. There are things I want to ask you.'

'It's too late for that. You had all the chance you needed to ask questions during the last week, but you were so busy being hurt and offended that you couldn't even begin to believe that there might be another explanation.'

'But I'm willing to listen now.'

'I told you: it's too late.'

Morgan turned to walk away but she caught his sleeve. 'You can't just leave,' Lyn protested in sudden panic.

'Why not? It's what you threatened to do time and again—after you finished telling me how much you hated me.'

'I was justified in the circumstances,' she said defensively. 'How did you expect me to feel? As it is I still only have your word for it that——' She stopped, biting her lip, not knowing what to think, who to believe.

'What a poor, mixed-up kid you are,' Morgan said sardonically. He gave a grin of wry self-mockery. 'Maybe I'll look you up in a few years' time—perhaps by that time you'll be a woman instead of a jealous schoolgirl.'

'But where will you go?'

He shrugged. 'Wherever I feel like.' His eyes grew cold. 'I don't have any ties.'

The coldness seemed to envelop Lyn's heart. She gazed at him numbly as he turned and began to walk away. Her emotions were still in dreadful turmoil, but as she watched him fear came to the fore and she ran after him. 'Morgan?' She gazed into his face, looking for some sign of softening, but his features were set into a hard mask.

'Well?'

'Please, I——' She tried to find words to tell him not to go but in the face of his coldness the words died. Instead she found herself saying, 'There are two questions I *have* to ask you. Please tell me why my father wanted me to come home.'

'I can't tell you that. You'll have to ask him yourself.' He looked at her expectantly but when she didn't speak said in harsh impatience, 'And the other question?'

'Why didn't you ever——,' She stumbled over the words, hesitated, became aware of all the people around them, and shook her head. 'It—it doesn't matter.'

Morgan looked at her bent head for a moment, his mouth twisting. 'Have a good trip,' he said shortly and strode away.

Lyn didn't run after him this time—there had been too much curtness in his voice for that. Almost immediately she went to sit in the nearest seat, her legs feeling suddenly weak, and so didn't see Morgan when he turned at the exit to glance back. When he saw that she had already moved away, his mouth set into a grim line and he walked on.

He had told her too much at once and too forcefully. Lyn's mind felt as if it couldn't take any more. The news of Claire's pregnancy had come as a particularly nasty shock. It had never even occurred to her that such a thing might happen. Her father was too old to start another family, for heaven's sake. But maybe he didn't think he was. Forty-seven wasn't that old, she supposed. But when it was your own father. . . She wondered what Morgan would do, where he would go. Maybe it wasn't too late. Maybe she could still find him. But her heart shrank from that look of cold contempt in his eyes. A look he had seen continuously in her eyes during the past week, she realised with a sudden feeling of horror. What if Claire had been lying, what if she'd made the most terrible mistake in believing her?

Tortured by doubts, Lyn flew home to England. She went back to the flat they had shared and waited for Morgan to telephone or write, afraid to go out in case she missed his call. After two weeks, when they would have been due back from their honeymoon, she rang her father at his office and asked if she could have lunch with him. But his voice was almost as cold and withdrawn as Morgan's had been. 'I'm sorry, Lyn, I'm very busy.'

'How about another day, then?' she suggested, trying to make her voice sound cheerful.

'I'm afraid I'm tied up indefinitely. What is it you want? If you've found a flat you like, let my solicitor know and he'll handle it,' he said brusquely.

'No, I—we haven't really looked yet. Has Morgan —did Morgan tell you. . .?' She stopped wretchedly.

'If you're trying to find out whether Morgan has told me that he's changed his mind about working with my company, then the answer's yes,' Jonathan Standish said shortly. 'And now, if you'll excuse me, I'm extremely busy.' And he put the phone down on her, a thing that had never happened to Lyn before in her life. She hadn't even had a chance to ask him what had happened to make him send Morgan to bring her home from Israel.

After two months of staying at home waiting for Morgan to call, Lyn forced herself to accept that he'd meant what he said and that he was through with her. And her father, too, had not called back. Lyn had never felt so lonely in her life. It was worse, far worse, than when her parents had split up. For a while she thought of going out to Australia to live with her mother, but from the letters and postcards she received it seemed that her mother and Walt were having an endless honeymoon, always travelling in or around Australia. Well, good luck to them; Lyn didn't intend to take her troubles out there and spoil things for them. She would just have to make out on her own.

Her father continued to pay her allowance, but Lyn stopped it, determined to stand on her own feet. But she desperately wanted to keep on the flat because that was where Morgan would look for her if he came back. So for a start she would have to get a job, Lyn decided on a wave of resolution. It wasn't as easy as she'd thought, because she'd had no training, but she managed to get a job eventually as a receptionist in a West End hairdressers. The pay wasn't very good but Lyn enrolled for a business studies course at evening college, hoping it would help her to get something better.

She worked hard that winter, trying to keep her mind occupied, but there were still long, lonely hours alone at the flat when she would open the wardrobe doors and run her hands over the clothes that Morgan had left there, or gaze at his photograph, wondering where he was. He'd said that maybe one day he would look her up; Lyn clung to that thought, but as the weeks passed hope began to die. Every day she expected to receive a letter from some solicitor saying that Morgan was suing for a divorce, but thankfully that didn't come either.

In January she got a new, better job in a small company and was soon taking on more responsibility. She felt better, not so down, but the ache of loneliness still filled her heart and she gave a cool refusal to the men who had nerve enough to ask her for a date. The phone almost stopped ringing, but, one cold night at the end of February when Lyn had gone to bed, its insistent sound dragged her from sleep.

Instantly alarmed, she grabbed up the receiver. 'Morga——'

She broke off as a woman said agitatedly, 'Mrs

French? This is Irene Wallis, your father's housekeeper. I'm afraid there's been an accident.'

'My father?' Lyn said on a hoarse note of fear. 'He's not—he's not dead?'

'I don't think so. I'm not really sure. I'm afraid I got rather flustered when the hospital phoned. It was a bad line, and it was difficult to understand, you see.'

'Which hospital was it?' Lyn asked urgently. Then, with difficulty, 'Does his wife know?'

'Oh, but she was with him in the car. They said something about her going into premature labour. Oh, dear, the poor things. I really——'

'Which hospital is it?' Lyn demanded again, her voice rising. 'I must go to them.'

'I have it written down here. Just a minute, let me get my glasses.' There were confused sounds on the line as Lyn waited with screaming impatience. 'Yes, it's the Hospital of the Sacred Heart,' the woman read out. 'I think that's what they said, but it was such a bad line.'

'I've never heard of it,' Lyn said in puzzlement. 'Are you sure it wasn't a hoax? It sounds so foreign.'

'Well, it would. It's Spanish.'

'Spanish?' Lyn's eyes widened in growing horror. 'Mrs Wallis, exactly where are they?'

'Why, they're in Tenerife, on holiday. I thought for sure you knew.'

'No, I—I didn't know.'

'Oh, dear, I'm sorry. Yes, Mrs Standish hadn't been feeling very well so your father took her to Tenerife for the winter, but they were due back next month so that she could have the baby in England.'

'Did the hospital give you a phone number?' Lyn asked, trying to think clearly through the fear for her father.

'Yes, I'll give it to you.'

Mrs Wallis repeated the number and Lyn spent a terrible half-hour trying to get through and then to get hold of someone at the hospital who could speak English and tell her exactly what had happened. It came as another shock to find that it hadn't been a straightforward car accident. It seemed that her father had suffered a heart attack at the wheel and that had caused the crash. He was now in intensive care.

Lyn phoned every airport in England but couldn't get a flight until seven in the morning. She was there hours too early, too consumed by anxiety to be able to sleep again, but there was a delay and it was early afternoon before Lyn finally got to the hospital in Tenerife. Her father was still in intensive care and Lyn was only allowed to look at him through the window of his room. Her heart jolted when she saw all the wires and tubes, but the doctor said that for him to have survived this far was a good sign, and he had every hope of a recovery.

'And now I expect you would like to see Señora Standish,' the doctor suggested. He frowned. 'But she is not your mother, surely?'

'No, she's my father's second wife.' Lyn hesitated. 'Has she—has she had the baby yet?'

'Not yet. We have tried to tranquillise her, but I think the baby will come soon,' the doctor told her in his precise English.

'Was she injured in the accident?'

'She has a sprained ankle and one arm is fractured, but it's the shock of the accident that will bring on the baby. And she is extremely worried about your father, of course. Come, I'll take you to her.'

Lyn hesitated, afraid that seeing her might upset Claire even more, but went with him because he expected it.

Claire, too, was in a private room and opened deep-shadowed lack-lustre eyes when the doctor told her she had a visitor. Fright came into them despite the tranquilliser as she saw Lyn, and she said, 'Jonathan?' on a high, terrified note.

'He's all right, he's holding his own,' Lyn hastened to assure her.

Her head fell back on the pillows as Claire gave a sobbing gasp of relief. 'I thought they'd sent for you because—because. . .'

Her hands tightened on the covers as a spasm of pain shot through her, and Lyn realised that she needn't have been concerned; Claire had far too much to worry about to even think of their feud.

A nurse came to find the doctor and he said, 'Perhaps you would like to stay with Señora Standish for a small while?'

Lyn sat down reluctantly in a chair by the bed, not knowing what to say. Claire gave a small moan, whether of pain or despair, Lyn didn't know. Trying to distract her, Lyn said, 'Please, can you tell me what happened? If you feel well enough. If—if it won't upset you too much.'

Claire turned to look at her, then sighed. 'We went out to dinner and were on our way back. It was raining.

We got a puncture and Jonathan got out to change the wheel. I remember he said the nuts were tight. I was worried about him but he wouldn't let me drive. We went on but he had another heart attack and the car went off the road on a bend.'

'*Another* heart attack!' Lyn exclaimed. 'Had he had one before?'

'Yes, while you were in Israel.' For a second her eyes flashed and Lyn caught a glimpse of the old Claire. 'He refused to tell you, of course. He was always trying protect you. He would have got a divorce years ago if he hadn't always been worrying about you.'

'Is that—is that why he sent Morgan to bring me home?' Lyn asked painfully, already knowing the answer.

'Yes. He wanted to see you settled, in case anything happened to him.'

And that's why he pushed Morgan into marrying me so quickly, Lyn realised. A great many things became clear in her mind now. She could imagine her father worrying over her future and that of his business; how he had seen Morgan as the answer to both problems. And Morgan, of course, had known and gone along with it. Not for money, because he hadn't wanted that lifestyle any more, but because he loved her.

Claire's eyes had closed again but she moved restlessly, obviously in great discomfort from her arm and ankle. Thinking that she might sleep if left alone, Lyn got up to go, but Claire reached out with her left hand and caught Lyn's sleeve. 'You'll stay? You won't leave us?' she begged urgently.

'No, of course not,' Lyn assured her unsteadily. 'I'll stay as long as you need me.'

'And you'll keep letting me know how Jonathan is?'

'Yes, I promise. I'm going to book into a hotel now but I'll come straight back.'

Claire went into labour later that day, but it was a long process and it was Lyn who held her hand for most of the time. And it was Lyn who told Claire that Jonathan Standish had regained consciousness and was feeling very much better, so that Claire was wheeled into the delivery-room with tears of relief rolling down her face.

They let Lyn sit with her father for a while, but he was very tired and had little to say except that he was glad she was there. He fell asleep and when he woke Lyn was able to tell him that he had a son, stifling the flash of jealousy when she saw the triumph and pleasure in his face. Maybe he had always wanted a son, she thought—but if so he had never let her see it.

With both of them convalescent, Lyn was kept very busy, buying clothes for the baby, bringing them the things they wanted, carrying messages to and fro, and packing up the villa they had taken. Luckily her father was well insured, so as soon as they were well enough they were flown home in an ambulance plane. Jonathan Standish had to go into hospital for a while longer, but Claire and the baby were allowed to go to the London house and Lyn went along to help on the journey.

The housekeeper, Irene Wallis, was waiting to welcome them, but, once Claire was settled in her room, she worriedly explained to Lyn that she had only been living in the house while the Standishes were away as a favour because they didn't want the place standing empty. 'I didn't mind doing it because my son has been away, but he's home now. I'm a widow, you see, and he's my only son so I don't want to be away when he's home. I'm really only employed during the day,' she added, looking at Lyn anxiously.

'Well, don't worry. I'm sure Mrs Standish will employ a live-in nurse to look after her and the baby,' Lyn soothed.

It fell to Lyn to ring round the agencies to find a nurse, but Claire was fussy and not everyone wanted to take on an accident case and a baby. And when the right person was found she unfortunately couldn't start straight away. Realising that she would have to cope until the nurse came, Lyn regretfully went to see her employers and explained the situation. The company had been very patient, but Lyn couldn't ask them for any more time off when she'd been there for such a short while. They were very good about it and even told Lyn to give them a ring when things had sorted themselves out, in case the position was still open.

Their confidence in her was a great boost to Lyn's morale. She went to the flat to pack some more clothes, and temporarily moved back into her old room at her father's house. She looked round the room, thinking that she had never expected to see it again, and remembering how she had last come into it on her wedding day, looking for something blue. For a moment then the thought of Morgan filled her mind and the bitter loneliness came flooding back. She tried so hard not to think of him, and looking after Claire and the baby and visiting her father left her with little enough time. But sometimes, at the most vulnerable moments, she would miss him so much that her heart literally ached with longing for him.

Her relationship with Claire was a nervous and embarrassed one on both sides, although necessarily an intimate one in the circumstances. They both felt self-conscious, and Lyn was sure that Claire would like to tell her to get the hell out, but until the new nurse came she was dependent on Lyn's help as she could do little for herself. In the evenings Lyn would sit with her while Claire had her meal, and then help her prepare for bed. 'Thank you. You're very kind,' Claire said one evening, a week or so after her return from Tenerife.

'That's OK. You don't have to keep thanking me,' Lyn said awkwardly. 'I'm glad to help.'

Claire turned to look at her. 'I can hardly believe that when you hate me so much. After all, I was the one who drove you and Morgan apart.'

Her face rather pale, Lyn said, 'You know that he left—that we split up, then?'

'Yes.' Claire leaned back against the piled up pillows with a sigh. 'Morgan came to tell me. He was so angry!' She shuddered at the memory. 'I thought he was going to kill me.'

'He *came* to tell you? You mean when you were in Tenerife?'

'No, last year, before we left. Some time in November, I think.' She paused and then said with difficulty, 'I'm sorry about what I did. But you made me so angry. I didn't mean to break you up. I only wanted to get back at you. I'm sorry, I——'

'You don't have to apologise,' Lyn said, her voice curt. She got to her feet. 'I've an idea it should be the other way round. I deserved what you did.' She turned away and switched out the overhead light. 'Goodnight. Call me if you need anything.'

Lyn took the supper tray into the kitchen, but then sat down at the table and put her head in her hands. Morgan had been in England, in London, and he hadn't been to see her. Bitter disappointment tore through her and Lyn burst into tears, crying her heart out in the empty kitchen.

The next morning was a busy one, thank goodness, as Lyn helped to get the room ready for the nurse's arrival the next day, fully expecting to leave herself as soon as the nurse had settled in. In the afternoon she took the baby to show to his proud father. 'The doctors have told me that I can come home in a few days if I promise to take it easy,' he told her. 'But I won't if it's going to be too much of a burden. I'll stay at a convalescent home or something.'

'You'll hate that. And surely you want to be with Claire?'

'Of course. But two invalids and a new baby are too much to ask any nurse to take on. I know we have Irene, as well, but even so. . .'

Lyn gave him a quizzical look. 'Are you asking me to stay on?'

'Will you?'

'Yes, all right.'

His eyebrows rose. 'You didn't even think about it.'

'You need me, so I'll stay,' she said with a shrug, but she felt grateful to be needed.

'And what about your dislike of Claire? I thought you hated each other.'

Lyn gave a small smile. 'I'm quite sure you've already discussed that aspect of it with her over the phone.'

'You've changed, Lyn,' he observed.

'Have I? It comes of being a working girl, I expect,' she said lightly.

'You had a job?'

'Yes, and I was taking a course in business studies at night school until. . .' She stood up. 'And I'll take it up again when you don't need me any more. Now I'd better take your son home to his mother before he gets hungry.' Leaning forward, she kissed her father on the cheek. 'So that's settled, then: you'll come home as soon as you can and I'll stay just until you can manage without me. Goodbye. Let me know when to collect you.'

'Lyn, wait. About Morgan. I——'

Her face tightened. 'I'd really rather not talk about him, if you don't mind. Goodbye.'

Jonathan Standish must have phoned Claire while Lyn was on the way home, because she already knew that he would soon be home and that Lyn was staying on. Claire was pathetically grateful and cried a little. She was still weak from the baby's birth, of course. Lyn tried to cheer her up by talking of the future when they would both be well again, and left her settled for the night feeling much happier.

Lyn had had to learn about new babies fast. During

the night she was in sole charge of changing and feeding, but at least the nurse would be moving in tomorrow, she thought with a grateful sigh as she prepared the ten o'clock feed in the nursery. He was quite a good baby, though, her little brother. Lyn lifted him out of his lace-embellished crib, cleaned him up, and held him in the crook of her arm as she gave him his bottle. He smelt of talcum powder and milk. And it was impossible not to love him. She was still feeding him when there was a ring at the front doorbell. Lyn frowned, looking at the clock and wondering who it could be. She put the baby down but he wailed, wanting his bottle. Afraid that he would wake Claire, Lyn wrapped him in a blanket, carried him down the hall, and opened the door.

It was raining outside and the man standing at the door was wearing a trench-coat but was bare headed. He turned as she opened it and Lyn almost dropped the baby in surprise. 'Careful.' Morgan stepped quickly forward as she clutched at the child.

For a moment they stood there, both of them holding the tiny baby between them, but their eyes gazing into one another's. Then Lyn tore her eyes away as she held the child more firmly. 'What do you want?' she said stonily. 'Claire has gone to bed. She——'

'I came to see you, not Claire.' Lyn swallowed, unable to speak, and he said, 'Could we go in? The baby will catch cold.'

She stepped out of the way and he came in and shut the door. 'I—I was just feeding him.' Turning, she went back upstairs to the nursery. Morgan quickly took off his mac and followed her, putting up a hand to push his damp hair off his forehead.

Lyn sat down and the baby gave a crow of content as she gave him his bottle again. Coming to stand beside her, Morgan smiled as he watched. 'What's his name?'

'James, and Claire doesn't want it shortened to Jamie.'

Morgan looked round for another chair but could only find a pretty, skirted stool, so he pulled that up and sat opposite her. 'Was this your nursery?' he asked.

'Yes. Claire had it redecorated, though.'

'She rang me this morning.'

Lyn gave him a quick glance, then put the empty bottle on the floor and lifted the baby on to her shoulder to gently rub his back.

'That seems to come naturally to you,' Morgan said with a grin, but then his face became intent as he said, 'Unfortunately I was out but Claire left a long message on the answerphone. And later there was another call from your father. They both seemed to think it was about time I came to see you.'

'*They* did?' she asked in raw hurt.

'Yes. I didn't get home until this evening, but then I came straight here.'

Getting to her feet, Lyn carried the baby over to his crib and laid him gently down, her face tender as she tucked him in and switched on the baby alarm. But the tension came back into her features as she said, 'You're living in England, then?'

'Yes, I've bought a farm in Wiltshire.'

Lyn had been bending to pick up the bottle but grew

still as he spoke, then straightened up. 'I see.'

She went to go past him but Morgan caught her arm. 'Lyn, come and sit down. Let's talk.'

Her heart thumping, she sat down again, sure that he'd come to ask for a divorce. But he reached out and took the bottle from her, set it down and held her hands, his eyes fixed on her face. 'I was going to give it six months,' he said, 'and then come to see you. I hoped that by then you would be—well, ready to try again.' Lyn's hands trembled convulsively and she quickly looked away. 'Lyn?'

'It—it's nothing. Go on.'

'Well, both Claire and your father told me very strongly today that I shouldn't wait any longer.'

'They both knew where you were, obviously. They never told me.'

'Did you ever ask them?' Morgan queried on a harder note.

'I tried to ask my father but he just said that you'd decided not to work for him. He made it clear how angry he was with me, so I couldn't ask him again. I had no one else I could ask,' Lyn said stonily.

Letting go her hand, Morgan put a finger under her chin so that he could see her face. 'You sound as though you missed me,' he said huskily.

Lyn's mouth tightened as she remembered and her eyes shadowed. 'Yes, I missed you.'

Morgan was silent for a moment, gazing at her, then took his hand away and said, 'Your father told me that you've been working and going to night school. Standing on your own two feet. And they both told me how marvellous you've been to them since the accident, how you've got over all your jealousy.'

Pulling her hand from his, Lyn stood up. 'So on their recommendation, on their—say-so, you're finally willing to come and see me. Perhaps even to take me back,' she said on a rising tide of anger. 'It was kind of you to come early and not make me sit out the full six months of pure hell not knowing where you were or whether you'd met someone else. *Thank you very much*!'

She turned away, her hands over her face, but Morgan was instantly beside her. 'Lyn! Oh, my darling girl. Don't cry. Please don't cry. If you knew how hard I've had to fight to keep away from you. How I've *longed* to be with you. I've yearned for you. Ached for you. There hasn't been a day that's passed that I haven't wanted to come to you and tell you how much I miss you and need you.'

'So why the hell didn't you?' Lyn demanded through tear-soaked eyes.

'Because you needed time to sort out your feelings. And I had to prove to you that I didn't need or want the job your father offered me—or his money.'

'You'd already told me that.'

'Yes, but did you really believe me? I didn't think so. And I wasn't even sure that you really loved me, you were so quick to believe the worst of me. I felt that we'd been rushed into marriage, and for all the wrong reasons. I wanted you to have time to decide for yourself what you wanted.'

'A-and now?'

Tilting her chin, he bent and kissed her lightly, his lips barely touching hers, and yet it was a kiss full of love. 'I want you to come and live with me and be my wife,' he said simply.

A blaze of happiness lit her eyes, but then they quickly shadowed and she looked away.

Morgan's brows drew into a frown but then they cleared and he said very firmly, 'I love you, Lyn. And I promise I'll never love anyone else but you.'

She went into his arms, then, tears of happiness running down her cheeks. 'Oh, why didn't you ever tell me that before? It made me so unsure, so uncertain . . . I loved you so much and I wanted to believe you, but I didn't think you loved me. You could have married anyone you wanted——'

'And I *did*,' Morgan broke in. 'I wanted *you*. Oh, my darling, surely you believe that?' Holding her a little away from him, he said forcefully, 'Every time we made love I was telling you how much I loved you. Every look, every touch. I thought you knew. Would it have been so wonderful for us if we hadn't been in love?' Lifting his hand he brushed a tear from her cheek. 'Maybe I was wrong, maybe I should have spelled it out, but I've never told any other woman that I loved her before, and I was saving that to tell you on our wedding night. I wanted that night to be special, something you would remember.' A rueful look came into his blue eyes. 'Instead of which. . .'

'I spoilt it all,' Lyn said wretchedly.

'Never mind. Forget the past. Let's just think about the future. We can start over and have another wedding night tomorrow.'

'Do you mean it?' Lyn put her arms round his neck and held him tight, her heart full of happiness. But then she drew back in dismay. 'Oh, but I can't! I have to stay here and look after Claire and the baby. And my father's coming home soon, so it could be weeks before——'

Morgan put his fingers over her lips. 'The nurse moves in tomorrow and it will be a few days before Jonathan comes home. So tomorrow night you'll be free.'

And twenty-four hours later, in their flat, he held his arms wide as she ran to him. They kissed fiercely and Lyn looked up at him in radiant happiness. 'Don't forget,' she said teasingly, 'I shall still expect ecstasy in twenty-five years' time.'

Morgan laughed in rich pleasure as he swept her up into his arms. 'Now and always, my little love—and especially now!'

MILLION DOLLAR JACKPOT
SWEEPSTAKES RULES & REGULATIONS
NO PURCHASE NECESSARY TO ENTER OR RECEIVE A PRIZE

1 Alternate means of entry: Print your name and address on a 3"×5" piece of plain paper and send to the appropriate address below.

In the U.S.	In Canada
MILLION DOLLAR JACKPOT	MILLION DOLLAR JACKPOT
P.O. Box 1867	P.O. Box 609
3010 Walden Avenue	Fort Erie, Ontario
Buffalo, NY 14269-1867	L2A 5X3

2 To enter the Sweepstakes and join the Reader Service, check off the "YES" box on your Sweepstakes Entry Form and return. If you do not wish to join the Reader Service but wish to enter the Sweepstakes only, check off the "NO" box on your Sweepstakes Entry Form. To qualify for the Extra Bonus prize, scratch off the silver on your Lucky Keys. If the registration numbers match, you are eligible for the Extra Bonus Prize offering. Incomplete entries are ineligible. Torstar Corp. and its affiliates are not responsible for mutilated or unreadable entries or inadvertent printing errors. Mechanically reproduced entries are null and void.

3. Whether you take advantage of this offer or not, on or about April 30, 1992, at the offices of D.L. Blair, Inc., Blair, NE, your sweepstakes numbers will be compared against the list of winning numbers generated at random by the computer. However, prizes will only be awarded to individuals who have entered the Sweepstakes. In the event that all prizes are not claimed, a random drawing will be held from all qualified entries received from March 30, 1990 to March 31, 1992, to award all unclaimed prizes. All cash prizes (Grand to Sixth) will be mailed to winners and are payable by check in U.S. funds. Seventh Prize will be shipped to winners via third-class mail. These prizes are in addition to any free, surprise or mystery gifts that might be offered. Versions of this Sweepstakes with different prizes of approximate equal value may appear at retail outlets or in other mailings by Torstar Corp. and its affiliates.

4. PRIZES: (1) *Grand Prize $1,000,000.00 Annuity; (1) First Prize $25,000.00; (1) Second Prize $10,000.00; (5) Third Prize $5,000.00; (10) Fourth Prize $1,000.00; (100) Fifth Prize $250.00; (2,500) Sixth Prize $10.00; (6,000) **Seventh Prize $12.95 ARV.

*This presentation offers a Grand Prize of a $1,000,000.00 annuity. Winner will receive $33,333.33 a year for 30 years without interest totalling $1,000,000.00.

**Seventh Prize: A fully illustrated hardcover book, published by Torstar Corp. Approximate Retail Value of the book is $12.95.

Entrants may cancel the Reader Service at any time without cost or obligation (see details in Center Insert Card).

5. Extra Bonus! This presentation offers an Extra Bonus Prize valued at $33,000.00 to be awarded in a random drawing from all qualified entries received by March 31, 1992. No purchase necessary to enter or receive a prize. To qualify, see instructions in Center Insert Card. Winner will have the choice of any of the merchandise offered or a $33,000.00 check payable in U.S. funds. All other published rules and regulations apply.

6. This Sweepstakes is being conducted under the supervision of D.L. Blair, Inc. By entering the Sweepstakes, each entrant accepts and agrees to be bound by these rules and the decisions of the judges, which shall be final and binding. Odds of winning the random drawing are dependent upon the number of entries received. Taxes, if any, are the sole responsibility of the winners. Prizes are nontransferable. All entries must be received at the address on the detachable Business Reply Card and must be postmarked no later than 12:00 MIDNIGHT on March 31, 1992. The drawing for all unclaimed Sweepstakes prizes and for the Extra Bonus Prize will take place on May 30, 1992, at 12:00 NOON at the offices of D.L. Blair, Inc., Blair, NE.

7 This offer is open to residents of the U.S., United Kingdom, France and Canada, 18 years or older, except employees and immediate family members of Torstar Corp., its affiliates, subsidiaries and all other agencies, entities and persons connected with the use, marketing or conduct of this Sweepstakes. All Federal, State, Provincial, Municipal and local laws apply. Void wherever prohibited or restricted by law. Any litigation within the Province of Quebec respecting the conduct and awarding of a prize in this publicity contest must be submitted to the Régie des Loteries et Courses du Québec.

8. Winners will be notified by mail and may be required to execute an affidavit of eligibility and release, which must be returned within 14 days after notification or an alternate winner may be selected. Canadian winners will be required to correctly answer an arithmetical, skill-testing question administered by mail, which must be returned within a limited time. Winners consent to the use of their name, photograph and/or likeness for advertising and publicity in conjunction with this and similar promotions without additional compensation.

9. For a list of our major prize winners, send a stamped, self-addressed envelope to: MILLION DOLLAR WINNERS LIST, P.O. Box 4510, Blair, NE 68009. Winners Lists will be supplied after the May 30, 1992 drawing date.

Offer limited to one per household.

LTY-H891

Coming Soon

Fashion A Whole New You in classic romantic style with a trip for two to Paris via American Airlines®, a brand-new Mercury Sable LS and a $2,000 Fashion Allowance.

Plus, romantic free gifts* are yours to Fashion A Whole New You.

From September through November, you can take part in this exciting opportunity from Harlequin.

Watch for details in September.

* with proofs-of-purchase, plus postage and handling

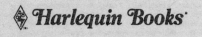